Dream
On

clearwater crossing

Dream On

laura peyton roberts

BANTAM BOOKS
NEW YORK • TORONTO • LONDON • SYDNEY • AUCKLAND

RL 5.8, age 12 and up
DREAM ON
A Bantam Book / February 2000

ISBN: 0-553-49298-5

Visit us on the Web! www.randomhouse.com/teens
Educators and librarians, for a variety of teaching tools, visit us at
www.randomhouse.com/teachers

Published simultaneously in the United States and Canada.

Bantam Books is an imprint of Random House Children's Books, a
division of Random House, Inc. BANTAM BOOKS and the rooster
colophon are registered trademarks of Random House, Inc. Bantam
Books, 1540 Broadway, New York, New York, 10036.

PRINTED IN THE UNITED STATES OF AMERICA

OPM   10 9 8 7 6 5 4 3 2 1

For Megan

Many are the plans in a man's heart, but it is the Lord's purpose that prevails.

Proverbs 19:21

From the desk of Principal Kelly
(Teachers: Please read in homeroom.)

Good morning, students:

As you know, the Wildcats' basketball season has come to an end. Please join me in extending congratulations to the team for never losing its fighting spirit!

The end of basketball is not the end of CCHS spirit, though. Spring sports are starting, and this Wednesday, March 10, there will be an informational meeting to kick off next month's cheerleading tryouts. If you are considering trying out, be sure to show up at the gym after school, as this meeting is required.

Finally, the cafeteria would like to announce a change to its menu. In response to student demand, Meat Loaf Mondays will now be Meatless Mondays. Enjoy.

Go, Wildcats!

One

"Meatless Monday," Peter Altmann griped, poking at the bean burrito on his tray. "What will they think of next?"

Jenna Conrad took a second bite of hers. "Meatless Tuesday through Friday, if we're lucky. This is a lot better than their meat loaf."

"Really?" Encouraged, Peter tried his. The tortilla was soft, the beans smothered with cheese and dripping a spicy red sauce. "Not bad," he agreed. He took a few more bites before pushing his tray to one side, ignoring the salad, rice, and brownie in the other compartments.

"You've got to see these pictures," he said, more interested in showing Jenna how much progress he'd made in planning the Junior Explorers' summer day camp. "I called the Park Service this morning, and they're supposed to get back to me about using the campground. I can't wait to get you up there to see it."

"Uh-huh. You going to eat that brownie?"

Peter laughed, happy that Jenna's appetite was finally returning. "No. Go ahead."

Spreading his photographs across the small stretch of table between them, he waited eagerly for her opinion. The day before he had wanted desperately to drive Jenna to the lake, to get her take on the deserted old Boy Scouts camp he'd selected, but Jenna had wanted to stay at the hospital with her family. Peter understood why she preferred to spend time with Sarah, when her youngest sister had come so close to dying after being hit by a drunk driver, but he had still been disappointed. He'd realized he'd been hoping that the moment Sarah came out of her coma, things could go back to normal between him and Jenna. Now, however, Jenna seemed as preoccupied with her sister's ongoing recovery as she'd been with her return to consciousness.

Sighing, he edged the pictures a little closer to his girlfriend. He missed the old days—the days when he and Jenna had done everything together. How much longer would it be, he wondered, before those times came back?

"What do you think?" he asked anxiously. "This one shows what's left of the old dock. I know it looks bad, but if the support timbers are still okay, we can build a new platform on them. The part people see will look brand-new."

Jenna put down her second brownie and pushed

her long hair back over one shoulder. "Is that Melanie?"

"Where?" Peter bent to peer at the photo she pointed to. Melanie Andrews smiled out through the broken window of the old shed, her face half lost in the shadows. "Oh, yeah. I forgot she was in there when I took that one. That's the shed I told you about. There's really nothing to it—the inside's just a shell—but somehow we'll have to make it into our office, storage building, and changing room. Maybe people will have ideas at the Eight Prime meeting this Thursday. You're going to be there, right?"

"Mmm," Jenna said noncommittally, pushing the photos back toward him. "I'm pretty busy right now." Her expression had turned sour, as if he'd said something wrong.

"I know. Are you going to the hospital right after school?" he asked quickly, fearing that her sudden change of attitude meant he'd been hogging the conversation again. He did care about Sarah—he cared a lot—but he was so consumed with the day camp that sometimes it was hard to think of anything else. Besides, he wanted Jenna to be as interested in the camp as he was. It just didn't seem right that she wasn't.

Jenna stood up, hoisting her backpack onto one shoulder. "Yes. So I'm going to the library now to try to finish my math homework. That will be one less thing I have to do tonight."

"Tell Sarah I said hi," he directed, watching uneasily as she walked off. Her brown hair swung freely across her back, shiny and beautiful, but her old jeans looked baggy and loose through the hips. She'd lost weight over the past few weeks.

"Hi, Peter. Hey, are those the pictures we took at the lake?" Melanie asked at his shoulder, startling him. "Can I see them?"

Dropping into Jenna's still-warm seat, she began poring over the photographs. "I can't believe you got them developed already."

"I took them to a one-hour place. I really wanted Jenna to see them."

Melanie nodded, glancing from shot to shot. "And did she like them?"

"I don't know."

She looked up, a puzzled expression in her green eyes. "How come?"

"It's just . . . she's still acting weird. I mean, one minute it's like everything's back to normal, and the next . . ."

"Worried about Sarah," Melanie said knowingly, returning to the pictures.

But Peter couldn't shake the feeling that it was more complicated. "Yeah," he sighed. "Or something."

"Oh, look at this one!" Melanie cried, holding it up and leaning close to give him a better view. Her blond hair smelled of spice and flowers. "This dock will be so cool once we fix it up!"

4

"Do you think so?"

"Oh, yeah. It's going to be great!"

"It *is* going to be pretty great," he said, reassured enough to smile again.

It was hard having Jenna so wrapped up with her family all the time. He was glad he at least had Melanie to keep him company.

"So, what's the verdict?" Ben Pipkin asked, grabbing an empty seat by Miguel del Rios just before the end of lunch. "I say Meatless Mondays rock!"

"You have taco sauce on your chin," Leah Rosenthal observed from across the cafeteria table.

Ben took the napkin she offered and wiped his face, ignoring the blush heating up his cheeks. What was a little hot sauce between friends? Especially when he had something much more important to discuss.

"Tomorrow's my birthday," he said happily. "Sixteen!"

Miguel gave him a close once-over. "And you don't look a day over twelve."

"Miguel!"

"He's just kidding. Happy birthday, Ben," said Leah.

"Yeah. You already told us, remember?" said Miguel.

"But I didn't tell you *this*," Ben said, gearing up for the best part. "I'm going to take the driving test on Saturday. By this time next week, I'll have my license."

"Do you, uh . . . do you really think you're ready?" Leah asked doubtfully.

"I know what you're thinking." He could guess, anyway. Whenever Ben was around Eight Prime, he had trouble with the simplest things. He was forever tripping, or spilling stuff, or finding some other way to make a mess. "But I'm really a good driver. My dad and I have been practicing for the past two weeks, and we're going to keep on practicing every night between now and Saturday. I have it in the bag," he said confidently.

"He got a hundred on the written part, you know," Miguel informed Leah in a teasing tone of voice. "Without even taking driver's ed!"

Ben had forgotten he'd told them that. "Well, I did! And I'll get a hundred on the driving part, too."

Miguel laughed. "Sure you will, hotshot. Next week you'll probably be *giving* the test."

"Please, Officer Ben," Leah played along in a syrupy accent, batting her eyelashes at him. "I really *do* know how to parallel park. If you could just move those nasty old cones a little farther apart . . ."

"Yeah, yeah," Ben grumbled. "You two sure are in a good mood today."

"They ought to feed us beans *every* day," Miguel quipped.

Leah broke up laughing and threw a crumpled napkin at her boyfriend.

Ben turned his attention back to the rest of the

cafeteria, wondering whether there was time to find Jesse before the bell rang. His roving gaze stopped dead, though, at the sight of a girl with long dark curls walking toward the trash cans.

Angela Maldonado, he sighed to himself. Every time he saw her, she seemed more beautiful. That Monday she wore a pink sweater with a matching beaded headband sparkling in her hair. He watched, mesmerized, as she bussed her tray, throwing away her milk carton, then dropping her silverware into the plastic tub.

"Do you think she's really going out with a basketball player?" he asked wistfully, repeating the rumor Mark Foster had told him.

"Who?" Leah asked, leaning forward. Her hazel eyes were wide with interest.

Ben felt his own eyes widen—with panic. Had he just said that out loud?

"No one! I mean, uh, Angela Maldonado. Not that it matters. That's just a story that's going around."

Miguel shrugged. "I have no idea."

"Me either," said Leah. "If you want to know, ask Angela."

Is she crazy? Ben could feel himself blushing, for real this time. *Not in a million years!*

"I don't want to know! I don't even care," he said loudly.

Miguel smiled sympathetically. "Or you could ask Melanie."

7

That idea, at least, was feasible. But Ben couldn't see himself trying it.

"I was just making conversation," he insisted with a weak smile. "Why should I care who Angela goes out with?"

He did, though. He cared a lot.

"Finally!" Courtney Bell huffed as Nicole Brewster let herself into the Bells' minivan. "If you'd made me wait here any longer, I would have run out of gas."

Nicole glanced from the full gas gauge to her best friend's impatient face. Courtney's red hair was mussed beneath a hastily shoved-on hat. Her gloved hands gripped the steering wheel as if the CCHS student parking lot were the start of the Indy 500.

"If you've been out here so long, why does the inside of this car still feel like a refrigerator?" Nicole's breath came out white with the question.

Courtney didn't answer, but she did adjust the heater as they drove off into a gathering storm. A cold snap had come in overnight, with the temperature continuing to plummet all day, and now light snow was predicted by nightfall. Nicole shivered in her down parka, glad she had thought to wear it.

"You know I'm still waiting to hear—" Courtney began.

"How about those cheerleading tryouts?" Nicole

cut in quickly. "Do you think I should go out again this year, or just give up?"

Ever since Nicole's double date with Guy Vaughn on Saturday night—the disastrous one where Courtney's old flame Jeff Nguyen had shown up with his new girlfriend—Nicole had done everything she could think of to avoid telling Courtney what had happened. All day Sunday she had managed to evade Courtney's calls, and at school that day she had slunk from place to place, pretending to be really busy. Courtney finally caught up with her after lunch, though, and Nicole had had to promise to reveal all after school. Unless, of course, she could distract her friend with something else . . .

"Why should I care?" Courtney asked, not falling for the ruse. "Are you going to tell me why Jeff hasn't called me, or what? Are we going out this weekend instead? What's going on, Nicole?"

"Well, I, uh, think Jeff was busy," Nicole stalled, going for understatement. The kind of news she had for Courtney didn't need to be blurted out all at once. "Are we going to your house or mine?"

"We're going to park on the side of the road in two seconds." Courtney's cheeks were flushed, and her green eyes had narrowed with ill-concealed anger.

Evasion wasn't working.

"Well, it's just that . . . it seems like . . . Jeff might

not be interested," Nicole got out, cringing in the passenger seat.

"*What?*" Courtney pulled to the curb and hit the brakes, staring Nicole down until she felt like a bug on a pin. "What do you mean, he's not interested? He seems pretty interested to me."

"It could be that he's just trying to bury the hatchet. You know. He's being *friendly*."

"No. I don't know." Courtney's expression was downright scary. "Enlighten me, Nicole."

"Jeff has a new girlfriend!" The words came out as if ripped from her lips. "Her name is Hope and he brought *her* on Saturday night."

The color drained from Courtney's cheeks, leaving them dead white.

"I didn't know what to do, Court," Nicole said pleadingly. "I knew I ought to tell you, but I knew you'd be upset. I didn't want to hurt—"

"This is unbelievable! I'm telling you, the guy's been flirting with me!"

"I know you *thought* that, but—"

"I'm not an idiot, Nicole. I know what I see." Courtney chewed her lips, scraping off the lipstick. "He is going to be so sorry."

"You're not going to do anything, are you?" It would be just like Courtney to make a huge scene and embarrass everyone. "I mean—"

"What does she look like?" Courtney demanded.

"Huh?"

"This girl. What does she look like? And what kind of name is Hope, anyway? I don't know *anyone* named Hope."

"Well, uh . . ." Nicole took a deep breath and dared to sit up a little straighter. Courtney was as angry as she had expected, but so far only at other people. Maybe, if Nicole played her cards just right, she could keep her friend's wrath focused where it belonged. "She looks a lot like you, actually. Red hair . . . pretty. Except that her eyes are blue. And she dresses a lot more conservatively."

Courtney snorted. "She'd have to, with a name like Hope."

"She goes to Guy's school, so I guess she's just more conservative all the way around."

Ozarks Prep was a private Christian academy. Revealing Hope's attendance there was enough to get her point across without telling Courtney that the four of them had gone to a Disney movie.

Courtney pushed against the steering wheel, stretching back in the driver's seat. Nicole could practically see her friend thinking as she worked through what she'd been told.

"This makes no sense," she announced at last. "Jeff breaks up with me, then goes out with someone who looks like me but doesn't know how to dress? Do you think Guy even told him I was still interested?"

"I doubt it," Nicole said timidly. "Jeff and Hope have been dating a few weeks."

11

Courtney slapped the steering wheel with both hands, making Nicole jump. "That explains it, then! He's trying to make me jealous."

"Well . . . I—"

"Think about it, Nicole. It's so obvious." Courtney checked for traffic, then pulled back onto the street. "I can't believe he wants to stoop to this. I thought he was more mature."

Nicole was pretty sure he *was* more mature. "I know it's weird that you and Hope are kind of twins," she ventured as the minivan barreled along. "But I, uh . . . I really think he likes her, Court."

"You're *supposed* to think that! Don't you see? Otherwise, what would be the point?"

Nicole scrunched up her face as she reflected on the evening she'd spent with Guy, Jeff, and Hope. *Maybe the point is that he likes her,* she thought, unable to put much stock in her friend's twisted logic. On the other hand, was it smart to contradict Courtney now, when she seemed so sure of her own explanation? Nicole had nothing to gain and everything to lose.

"It's just . . . if he was trying to make you jealous, wouldn't he pick someone who looks nothing like you? I don't get that part at all."

Courtney shook her head. "No, his way is worse. Because if she looks just like me, why not me? If you don't get it, I don't have time to explain it to you, Nicole."

Fine, thought Nicole, convinced she had done her duty. Actually, she'd just as soon Courtney *didn't* explain it to her.

"Jeff will be sorry, though. I can tell you that. All he had to do was apologize, and I was ready to take him back. Now I'll make him wish he had never started this."

Nicole smiled weakly, not wanting to draw Courtney's ire her way. After all, she was relieved her friend hadn't blamed her.

Still . . .

Part of her couldn't help wondering if she'd be sorry next.

Two

The first snowflakes started to fall as Leah and Miguel pulled into the hospital parking lot after school on Tuesday. They parked and watched from behind the windshield as the tiny puffs of white floated down to the pavement.

"Maybe it's an omen," Leah teased. "All hail Dr. del Rios!"

Miguel cocked one dark eyebrow. "I like the sound of that. It has a definite ring."

Leah laughed. "Yeah? Well don't expect to get used to it anytime soon," she said, shoving him playfully.

"Are you sure you want to wait for me?" he asked as they walked toward the lobby doors. "What are you going to do for three whole hours?"

"I wouldn't miss this for anything," she replied with a grin. "Your first day as an intern! I'll visit with Jenna and Sarah awhile, and then I'll find a nice quiet corner somewhere." Reaching behind her, she patted the backpack hanging from her shoulder. "I brought homework."

Miguel hesitated, then dropped a good-bye kiss on her cheek. "Okay. I'm just going to . . ." He nodded toward the elevators. "I think it will be better if I show up by myself. First day and all."

"All right. Knock 'em dead." Leah covered her mouth as she realized what she'd just said. "Oh, no! You know what I mean."

Miguel winked as the elevator doors closed between them. "I'll do my best."

Leah hummed happily while she waited for another elevator. Having Miguel working at the hospital seemed like a dream come true. For one thing, it was a great opportunity, a chance for him to find out if becoming a doctor was really what he wanted. But even better, it got him away from his previous job painting office buildings—and his attractive former supervisor, eighteen-year-old Sabrina Ambrosi. Leah had started obsessing about Sabrina from almost the very first second she'd seen her, even though Miguel had assured her over and over that he and Sabrina were only friends.

They're only friends now! she thought triumphantly. Maybe it was silly, but when Miguel had told her on Sunday night that he'd quit his job with the Ambrosis, she had almost cried with relief.

"You quit? For real?" she'd repeated disbelievingly. "What did Sabrina say?"

"About what?"

"About you leaving!"

"Oh. Not much, I guess. Her father's the one I mostly talked to. He said I'd be welcome back anytime. Maybe even this summer, if I have time to do both things."

We'll worry about summer when it comes, Leah thought now as the elevator doors opened and she stepped in. *Today, I'm just going to enjoy this.*

Leah didn't see Miguel when she got out on the second floor, but she found Jenna in Sarah's room, exactly as she had hoped.

"Hi, how's the patient?" she asked softly, sticking her head through the open doorway.

Jenna quickly put a finger to her lips. Rising from the chair beside Sarah's bed, she slipped out into the hallway with Leah, closing the door behind her.

"She just fell asleep," Jenna whispered. "She sleeps a lot. Should we go down there?" she asked, pointing to a windowed alcove at the end of the hallway.

There was a sofa beneath the windows, but neither girl sat down. Instead they stood and watched the snow falling softly outside.

"The weather's been so nice lately, I was starting to think winter was over," said Jenna.

"You know March. It usually packs one last punch."

Leah turned her back on the window and dropped onto the vinyl couch cushions. "So how is Sarah? I would think it's normal for her to sleep. It's not like there's much else to do here."

"Right. No, it's fine." Jenna sat down too. "We were really, really lucky."

"I'll say."

When the youngest member of the Conrad family had been hit by a car while walking home from school, it had seemed her hope of surviving was slim. Sarah had sustained a ruptured spleen, severely broken ribs, and a broken leg. Ultimately more frightening, however, was the diffuse brain injury that had kept her in a coma for two weeks. Sarah's doctor had told the family that if she lived there was a very real—and unpredictable—chance of brain damage.

"And is she . . . is everything coming back all right?" Leah asked.

Jenna nodded. "She doesn't remember the accident, or anything right before it, but Dr. Malone says that's pretty standard. Her speech is all right, and so is her vision. I guess those are two of the more common problems. They're a little worried about how she'll walk, but she *will* walk. She's not paralyzed or anything."

"I guess any time you break a leg that badly . . ."

"It's not the leg, it's her brain. I mean, the leg still needs to heal, but . . . we'll just have to wait and see."

Jenna shook her head slightly, then smiled. "I know this sounds weird, but even seeing Sarah limp will be the most beautiful sight in the world. What difference does that make compared to losing her?"

"None," Leah agreed wholeheartedly. She imagined Miguel in an accident, needing to use a cane or something. "If anything, it will probably bring you closer."

"Exactly. And we're not even positive she'll have a permanent problem." Jenna's expression was calm and happy, perfectly resigned.

"That's great, Jenna. We're all so glad for you. Everyone was going crazy worrying, especially Peter. I can't wait for the Eight Prime meeting at Jesse's house this week. It'll be just like old times now that everything's back to normal."

Jenna's smile seemed to fade just a little. Her lips still curved happily, but her eyes were no longer involved. "Yeah. Thanks."

"I mean, I know Sarah's still here in the hospital, but she's definitely going to be okay now. Right?"

"Right."

So why didn't Jenna seem more enthusiastic?

"There's not something you're not telling me, is there?"

"No, of course not." Jenna looked surprised. "What makes you say that?"

"Nothing. It's just . . . Never mind." Leah shook off the intuition of a moment before. Jenna seemed perfectly happy now.

"Well, I guess I'll go down to the lobby and get some homework done," Leah said. "I have a ton."

"I know! Are the teachers on some kind of tear lately? I think mine had a secret meeting or something."

Leah laughed. "Mine must have been there too. I'll see you in school tomorrow, all right?"

"Sure." Jenna extended a hand for Leah to pull her to her feet. "What thrill will it be tomorrow, I wonder? Wheatless Wednesday?"

The girls stifled giggles as they walked back down the hallway, but by the time Leah stepped into the elevator she felt uneasy again. Jenna seemed almost back to normal, but there was something Leah couldn't put her finger on. Just a nagging feeling, a sense that something wasn't quite right.

Was Jenna hiding something about Sarah after all? Was there something about her condition she didn't want people to know? Leah felt almost certain there must be. She punched the Lobby button with a growing sense of worry.

I guess she has a right to her privacy. Besides, I'm probably imagining things. She said Sarah was fine, and I don't think Jenna would lie.

Leah stepped out into the lobby, somewhat reassured.

On the other hand, it couldn't hurt to keep my eye on things for a while. If Jenna needs a friend, I want to be there for her.

19

"Are you paying attention, Vanessa?" Sandra Kincaid's dark eyes signaled her growing irritation with the captain of CCHS's cheerleading squad. "Or is this a little too much for you to take in?"

The school's eight cheerleaders sat in a semicircle on the polished gymnasium floor while their coach stood to address them, a metal clipboard in her hand. Tiffany Barrett cackled derisively, and under cover of the noise Tanya Jeffries leaned over to whisper to Melanie.

"What *she* can't take in is the fact that she's not in charge of tryouts. I can't wait for Vanessa to graduate."

"Yeah, and take Tiffany with her," Melanie whispered back. "Maybe then we can finally be a team."

When Melanie had joined the squad as the school's first-ever sophomore cheerleader, she'd held high hopes about what being a cheerleader would do for her morale. None of those dreams had panned out, though, and Vanessa's constant sniping at her had been the most depressing part of all. Self-absorbed, superficial Tiffany was no fun to be around either, but at least she didn't seem to have it in for Melanie. Thankfully, however, both Vanessa and Tiffany were graduating, along with Sue Tilford and Cyndi White. There would be four new girls on the squad next year—more if any of the younger cheerleaders didn't re-earn their places.

"I heard every word you said," Vanessa told the coach in a mocking tone of voice.

"Good." The way Sandra turned her attention from Vanessa back to her notes made Melanie think she wouldn't be sorry to lose a couple of seniors either. Ever since Sandra had taken over responsibility for the squad, she and Vanessa had been locked in a power struggle that showed no sign of ending before graduation.

"As I was saying," Sandra continued, "tomorrow's meeting will be strictly informational. The girls who turn out will sit in the bleachers and listen to a brief presentation, followed by a question-and-answer session."

"Question!" Lou Anne Simmons's arm shot into the air. "What about the guys who turn out?"

Sandra looked taken aback. "Did any guys come out last year?"

"Well . . . no."

"Then we'll cross that bridge if we come to it."

Sandra began passing out sheets of paper covered with tiny type. "This is the practice schedule for the next few weeks. All the candidates will get one tomorrow. As you can see, there will be a number of open practices for people to learn the cheer and required dance, and you girls will be teaching them. What's not on the sheet, however, are the practices that involve only us. The first one will be this Thursday, then again on Friday. The first open practice is

21

Saturday, and I want to be sure you have your routines dead perfect before you teach them to anyone else."

Melanie's arm went up. "But we don't need to be here tomorrow, do we? I mean, not for the informational meeting."

"Of course you need to be here," said Sandra, raising her eyebrows. "How would it look if you weren't? Besides, I think we'll do a couple of cheers to set the mood. Now, if you'll all just read down this schedule with me . . ."

Melanie kept her eyes on the paper as Sandra continued describing the obligations the squad would be expected to fulfill in the coming weeks, but she didn't see a word. Normally she appreciated Sandra's seriousness, her well-intentioned efforts to turn the CCHS squad into a force to be reckoned with, but that day all she felt was trapped.

How am I ever going to get downtown now? she thought despairingly. *She's got us tied up the whole week!*

Ever since Melanie had finished reading her mother's high-school diary on Saturday, the questions it had raised burned in her mind. Her own life had become a process of going through the motions, watching herself from a distance while the largest part of her brain worked on unraveling her mother's past. More than anything else, Melanie wanted to know if Tristyn had married her high-school boyfriend, Trent Wheeler, or if something had prevented that union. And if her mom *had* married Trent, what had become of him? Had he died? Had they divorced?

Not knowing was eating her up, but, for a lot of reasons, Melanie didn't want to ask anyone in her family. Unfortunately, however, Internet sessions had failed to turn up marriage records. On Monday, she had ridden the bus to city hall after school, only to find out that the person she needed to talk to had called in sick.

Now I'm not going to be able to get down there for the rest of the week. Not before they close, anyway. They were closed on weekends, too. *This stinks!*

Maybe I'll cut class. Although it didn't seem like the brightest possible plan to march into city hall while playing hooky.

Cut practice, then. Which might not be smart either, if she wanted Sandra to put her on the squad again next year.

"Any questions?" Sandra asked, jolting her back to the present.

Yeah, Melanie thought sullenly. *When are we supposed to have a life?*

This isn't exactly what I imagined, thought Miguel, staring down at the children's book in his hand.

23

I can't believe they're paying me for this. Glancing at the title, he made a quick decision and shoved it onto a shelf in the rolling library cart he was straightening.

When he had reported to work an hour before, the nurse at the desk had informed him that Dr. Wells, his supervisor, was in surgery. "He'll probably stop by later, but in the meantime, go ahead and dive in. Walk around, get familiar with where things are. Oh, and you're supposed to wear this," she'd said, handing a folded blue item over the counter.

Miguel had found himself holding a new scrub top with an official-looking tag that identified him as MIGUEL, STUDENT VOLUNTEER.

"I know you're not strictly a volunteer," the nurse had explained, "but if we put 'student intern' on there, people would think you're in medical school, and we don't need that kind of confusion. You understand."

"Sure," he'd said, although now his being confused with a medical student didn't seem too likely. He doubted many of them spent their hospital time on the urgent, life-or-death task of rearranging library books in the playroom, and he couldn't really see anyone yanking him away from *The Wizard of Oz* to ask him to save little Timmy.

The problem was, he didn't know what else to do.

There weren't any kids in the playroom to entertain at the moment. The real staff was all busy, so there was no one to give him a clue. He didn't know how to do anything medical, and he couldn't exactly barge into sick kids' rooms and introduce himself. Could he?

It could be worse, he reminded himself. *I could be working with Sabrina today.*

Miguel could still barely believe the way she'd behaved Sunday night, when he had come to her house to tell her father he was quitting. At first she'd just seemed worried that she'd upset him somehow. But then he'd found out the real reason she cared: Sabrina was interested in him for more than his office-painting services.

Well, I set her straight, he reassured himself, wiping his suddenly sweaty brow. *At least I hope I did.*

He'd told her clearly that he loved Leah, that Sabrina could never be more than his friend. But had she gotten the message? She'd listened, but she hadn't seemed too discouraged.

It's just a very good thing that I'm here at the hospital now. Sabrina can't get her hopes up if she never sees me. And if I had to have that temptation in front of me every day—

"Oh, good," said a voice behind him, startling him out of his thoughts. "I found you. Are you just about done with that?"

Miguel turned to see a man with a crew cut wearing full scrubs, a stethoscope looped over his shoulder.

"Yes. Yes, I'm done," said Miguel, scrambling to his feet. "Are you Dr. Wells?"

The man threw back his head and laughed. "Right. No, I'm just a lowly nurse. Most of the education, all of the hours, none of the credit. Name's Howard." He held out a hand for Miguel to shake.

"Pleased to meet you. I'm Miguel."

"Yeah, I know. Listen, if you're not doing anything, I could use some help with a kid on my shift."

"Sure! You name it," Miguel said eagerly.

"His name's Zachary, he's nine, and he's not feeling so great right now." Howard gestured toward the book cart. "Maybe you could read him something."

"Absolutely." Miguel's eyes skimmed over the titles. "Do you know what he'd like? Does he have any favorites?"

"It doesn't matter. Anything to take his mind off puking. And if you can get him to fall asleep, even better."

Quickly Miguel grabbed a couple of mysteries off the end of a shelf. Then he added a picture book, a book of cartoons, and an adventure story about two boys lost in the woods.

"All right, already. If he's not asleep after all that,

we have bigger problems than I think," said Howard, motioning for Miguel to follow him.

They went down a corridor, stepping into a room with an open door.

"Zach? How ya doing, bud?" Howard asked. When he'd been talking to Miguel, Howard's voice had been brisk, even flip. Now it was soft and sympathetic. "Any better yet?"

Walking to the bed, he laid a hand on Zachary's forehead, then began checking the numerous monitors and IVs attached to the small boy. Zach lay in the middle of the tubes and wires like the small center of an octopus, his brown eyes huge with anxiety.

"Howard, I feel like I'm going to barf again."

"It's okay if you do. You have a pan right here, and if you miss it, that's okay too. You just hang in there, Zach. You'll feel better soon."

Zach gripped the blue plastic pan on his chest as if afraid it might run away. Howard tousled the boy's thin brown hair, making it stand up in spikes. "You're a good kid. Look, I brought someone to meet you."

Turning back toward the door, Howard motioned for Miguel to come in closer. "His name's Miguel and he's new here, so maybe you can help teach him how we do things."

"All right."

Zach strained to sit a little higher in the bed, presumably to get a better look. Miguel took a few steps forward, shy under nine-year-old scrutiny.

"Are you a doctor or a nurse?" Zach asked curiously.

"Neither. I'm still in high school."

"What are you doing here?"

"I'm just helping out. I can read you a story, if you want some company."

"What books did you bring?"

"I'm sure he has something you'll like." Howard grabbed a chair from near the door and moved it over to the bedside, motioning for Miguel to sit. "I'll come back later and see how you're getting on." With a final tweak to the extra blanket covering Zach's feet, Howard was gone.

"So, I, uh . . . Howard told me you're nine."

"How old are you?" Zach demanded. His eyes were so large and round, he reminded Miguel of an owl with spiky top feathers. His skin was as pale as a night creature's, too, suggesting a protracted illness.

"Seventeen. Almost eighteen."

"That's pretty old."

Miguel smiled. "Practically over the hill. So what do you say?" he prompted, holding up the books he had brought. "Can I interest you in a story?"

Zach looked them over.

"That one," he decided, pointing to the lost-in-the-woods adventure with two boys on the cover. "I'm way too sick to hear about girls."

Miguel choked back a laugh as he opened the book. Not only were he and Zach going to get along fine, the kid's grip on his barf pan was already getting looser.

Three

"First of all," Sandra Kincaid's voice boomed through the gym speakers Wednesday, "I'd like to welcome everyone who came to our meeting. What a big turnout!"

The bleachers rustled in nervous agreement.

"I'll say," the girl to Nicole's right muttered, sounding nearly as tense as Nicole felt.

Except that she couldn't be. Not even close, Nicole thought, scooting forward to the edge of her bench. *I'm so scared I can't even feel my feet.*

Working up the nerve just to be seen entering the building had been a major achievement. On her way up the bleachers, her legs had started going numb, as if she were walking on rubber stilts. She'd done her best to keep them from wobbling, wondering if the other girls were checking her over—her clothes, her face, her makeup—and laughing at her for thinking she had a chance. Even now, as she sat in the relative anonymity at the center of the crowd, Nicole's stomach felt shaky, and she'd developed a flutter in her right eye. If she was this scared at the first meeting, how was she ever going to hold herself together long enough to audition?

Especially when I didn't even make the cut last year . . .

Was it worse to be ridiculed for trying out and not making the squad two years in a row, or to go through her whole life wondering if she could have been a cheerleader if she'd just tried one more time?

"Did everyone get a schedule?" Sandra asked, holding up a sheet of paper. "If not, look at your neighbor's for now and be sure to pick one up on your way out."

Nicole's hands tightened on the copy in her lap, but she didn't look at it. Her eyes were glued to the scene on the gymnasium floor.

Three rectangular tables had been pushed into a line. All eight cheerleaders sat behind them facing the bleachers, four on either side of the coach. Sandra stood at a microphone in the center, seemingly trying to make eye contact with each of the hundred girls in the crowd.

No, it has to be more than a hundred, thought Nicole, feeling sick. *It's too many, that's for sure.*

She tried to do the math—a hundred girls divided by eight spots—but it didn't go in evenly and she couldn't concentrate at all.

Besides, there could be a hundred and fifty girls here.

And only four spots, she suddenly realized. Lou Anne, Angela, Melanie, and Tanya were all underclassmen; they were sure to come back next year. Nicole almost groaned aloud.

"Now, if you'll just follow me as we read through this . . ." Sandra began going over the schedule, emphasizing the important dates and explaining the types of clothing and equipment that would be needed at each practice: shorts, sweats, pom-poms, a blank audiotape . . .

Nicole suddenly noticed that the girl on her left had pulled out a pen and was using it to circle important points. Her heart lurched in her chest. Should she be taking *notes*?

A scan of the girls in her immediate area revealed that at least half of them were. Nicole rummaged through her backpack in a panic, desperate not to fall behind in the first ten minutes of the very first meeting.

But there was really nothing to write. Pencil hovering over her schedule, she doodled nervously down the margin, her eyes on the cheerleaders again.

Melanie was seated next to Tanya at one end of the tables, so obviously sure she belonged there she even looked a little bored. She clearly didn't harbor a doubt in the world about her ability to beat every one of the girls in the stands.

Nicole, on the other hand, had never felt more insecure.

How would it feel to be that confident? she wondered enviously. *To sit behind one of those tables like an undisputed queen?*

If she didn't make the squad this time, she'd never get to find out.

"Okay," Mr. Pipkin said, checking the parking brake box on his homemade driving examiner's list. "Now how about the headlights?"

"Lights! Right!" Ben replied snappily, twisting the end of a wand on the steering column. Water sprayed from two spouts on the hood, running in rivulets down his father's windshield.

"Those are the windshield wipers, Ben," Mr. Pipkin said tightly. "I thought we ironed that out yesterday."

Thinking quickly, Ben pulled on the wand he'd just turned. The wiper blades swept back and forth, clearing two big swaths. "I thought the glass looked dirty."

"The three gallons you squirted up there yesterday didn't do the trick? I don't want to fill that thing again."

Moving more cautiously, Ben successfully located the lights, demonstrating both high and low beams. He knew exactly where they were, so why did he always go for the wipers? It was a mental block or something.

Mr. Pipkin made another check mark. "You know

they're going to ask you this stuff when you take the test. You don't want to lose such easy points before you even start driving."

"I know. I'll get it. I mean, I've *got* it. I just get ahead of myself and then . . . Can we start driving now?" The engine was already running, and if he could just get onto the street, Ben knew he would be okay.

His father adjusted his seat belt. "All right. What's the first thing you do before you pull away from the curb?"

"Signal," Ben said with relief. At least he was sure about that. Setting the left signal blinking, he pulled away from the curb.

"Wrong!" his father cried. "You have to look first, Ben! What if a car had been coming? You think people stop just because you signal? Or what if there had been a kid on a bicycle or something? You just killed him!"

"No one was coming . . . ," Ben began weakly.

Mr. Pipkin glanced behind them. "Stop the car."

Ben applied the brakes so abruptly that he and his father both rocked forward in their seats. The car stopped in the middle of the residential street.

His father took a few deep breaths. "I don't mean to yell at you, son. But you have to realize how serious this is. I'm not exaggerating when I say you could kill someone, and that someone could be you."

34

Ben hung his head, focusing on his birthday wristwatch through a film of unshed tears. His father so rarely raised his voice that he knew he had really messed up.

"I hate to say this," Mr. Pipkin went on, "but I think you were doing better last week. Maybe we're overpracticing."

Ben's shoulders dropped another inch. He *had* been doing better then, but how could his current troubles be caused by too much practice? More likely it was his father's new game of pretending to be a driving examiner.

"I just have to pay more attention," Ben said. "I really do know what to do. It's just that you're sitting there with that clipboard now, and there's all these details to remember and—"

"There *are* a lot of details. And when you take the test, a total stranger will be in this seat, making you twice as nervous. I know you're sixteen now, but I'm starting to think we're rushing this. Why not take a few days off? It will give us both a chance to rest."

"*What?* No! I don't *want* to rest! It's already Wednesday, and I'm taking the test Saturday."

"You know, maybe that's not such a good idea either. Why don't we take our time and do a few more weeks of practice? After all, what's the hurry?"

"What's the hurry?" Ben repeated, horrified. "Just that I already told everyone I know that I'm taking the test this weekend. If I don't have a license on Monday, I'll look like a total fool!"

Mr. Pipkin toyed with his pencil a moment, then looked directly at his son. "Not as much of a fool as you'll look like if you take the test and *still* don't have a license."

Ben felt weak at the mere thought. *No. I have to take the test, and I have to pass.*

"Please, Dad," he begged. "Give me another chance. You know I can do this—you've seen me."

"You can drive us around the block," Mr. Pipkin said. "But that's about all I have left for tonight. And if you make any more dangerous maneuvers—"

"I won't," Ben promised quickly. There was no good way that sentence could end.

His hands kept a death grip on the wheel as he inched down the darkening street, alert for the first sign of a hazard. The headlights seemed to cut a path for him to follow, even though it was still light enough to see children in the yards to either side. Reaching the first corner, Ben checked for traffic, put on his signal, and slowed nearly to a stop before he made the turn. Every movement was expertly smooth.

"Ben?"

"What!"

"It's okay to breathe some too."

* * *

"There you are!" Peter rushed forward as Jenna walked into the Joneses' den on Thursday night, the last member of Eight Prime to arrive. Closing the small-paned glass door behind her, he breathed a sigh of relief. "I was starting to wonder if you were coming."

"My dad got home late with the car."

"You should have let me drive you. I could have just swung by your house."

"Oh, well."

Jenna glanced around the den as if trying to get her bearings. Leah, Melanie, and Nicole sat together on the sofa, looking at the book Jenna had given Peter about running day camps; Miguel and Ben stood talking by a plate of cheese and crackers; and Jesse and his twelve-year-old stepsister, Brittany, hovered near a lopsided cake at the end of the bar, whispering back and forth.

"What's the cake for?" Jenna asked.

"Ben's birthday was Tuesday." Eagerly Peter propelled her forward into the room. "Hey, everyone, Jenna's here. We can get started now."

"Are you in a hurry or what?" Jesse said, walking over to meet them. "First we want to do the cake."

"Oh. All right," Peter said sheepishly. "I guess I was just so excited to tell you guys what I've learned . . ."

Jesse laughed. "Well, Brittany's pretty excited

37

about serving her first homemade cake. It'll only take a minute."

Moving back to the bar, where his little sister still waited, Jesse called for the group's attention. "If everyone could look over here a minute . . . Come on up, Ben."

An embarrassed but pleased-looking Ben was dragged to the front of the room by Miguel, while the rest of the group serenaded him with "Happy Birthday." Peter lip-synched along with the others, hoping no one would notice. Not being able to sing was always a burden on birthdays.

Ben was blushing profusely by the time the song had ended. "You guys didn't have to do all this. Did you make it yourself?" he asked Brittany.

"Jesse and I did," she said, nodding proudly. "It wasn't even that hard!"

Jesse sported a bit of a blush himself as he lit the sixteen candles. "If I can't follow the directions on a box by now, I'll be in big trouble senior year."

"The frosting came in a can," Brittany confided. "But it's really good."

The candles were admired, then blown out. Eventually everyone was holding some cake on a paper plate.

"Do, uh, do you guys want to get started now?" Peter asked, dying to move things along. He didn't want to rush Ben's big moment, but he had some news of his own he was just about bursting with.

"Brittany's staying for the meeting," Jesse announced abruptly, looking around as if someone might argue.

"Fine. Although you might be bored," Peter warned her. "We have a lot to do tonight."

Brittany shook her head. "I don't mind. I can always have seconds on cake."

At last everyone was seated, looking expectantly at Peter. He couldn't wait to get started.

"All right! By now you all know that there's a potential site for the Junior Explorers day camp. Who's got the pictures?"

"Got them!" Leah held up the packet that had been going around.

"If you haven't already seen them, take a look," Peter urged. "If you have, you know the place needs work, but—"

"I'll say!" Nicole interrupted, setting aside her sliver of cake. "It doesn't even look like a camp. It doesn't look like much of anything."

"Not yet," Peter admitted. "But it's a great location, and here's the best part: We can get it cheap! I talked to the Park Service again this afternoon, and they've tentatively agreed to let us have it for a dollar a day, provided we fix it up. Chris and I will meet them Monday after school and try to finalize an agreement. That is," he said, pausing hopefully, "if that's what you all want to do."

Jesse had taken the photos from Leah and was

flipping through them. "Why do you care what we think? It's your camp, right? You should do whatever you want."

Peter glanced at Jenna, hoping she'd speak up for him, but she seemed lost in the meeting notes she was taking.

"Well . . . not exactly. When the group talked about this before, I got the impression you all might want to help. It's going to take a lot of money to fix up the campground, and Chris isn't going to be around much this summer. I'll need help watching the kids."

"I'll be a counselor," said Ben. "It'll be fun."

"Thanks, Ben." Peter tried not to envision spilled paint and broken legs. "But if we run all summer, like I'm hoping, you'll want time to do other things too. Maybe if we can rotate among everyone . . ."

"Shouldn't we worry about first things first?" asked Miguel. "I thought we were going to plan the St. Patrick's Day sucker sale."

"Right." Excited by the Park Department's offer, Peter had hoped to seal the group's commitment to the camp that evening, but the real reason they were there was to figure out how to sell a few hundred green suckers Ben had mistakenly purchased for Valentine's Day. "That's next Wednesday. Any ideas how we should do it?"

Miguel shrugged. "I think we have to take them back to school."

"We can't!" Nicole protested. "Everyone there saw them last month. We'll be laughed right out of town."

"It's not ideal," said Melanie. "But I agree with Miguel. Our best chance of selling them is during the school day, when people are most concerned about wearing green."

"Maybe we could make them look different some-how," Jenna suggested.

Everyone looked at her expectantly.

"I don't know how," she admitted.

"Hey, I have an idea!" said Leah. "Let's make them wearable! We can tie little bows around the sticks and sell them with a pin, like corsages. That way, if people forget to wear green, they can pin one on and still have it covered."

"That's a good idea!" Ben exclaimed enthusiasti-cally. "And for the guys, we can make boutonnieres!"

"I suppose on some of them we could just wrap the stems with that green floral tape," said Leah. "I have a feeling the girls are our best shot, though."

"Definitely," Jesse said with conviction.

A few more minutes of discussion followed before the group agreed to go with Leah's idea and disguise the suckers as corsages.

"I think my mom has some of that green tape lying around from a crafts thing she was doing," Leah said. "We might have a roll of ribbon, too."

"I know we have a bunch of old ribbon," said Jenna. "Why don't you and I decorate the suckers?"

"Do you need any help?" Melanie asked. "I'm pretty busy this week, but—"

"That's okay," Jenna said quickly. "It will give me something to work on at the hospital."

"What will we do with the ones that we don't sell at school?" Nicole wanted to know.

"Dump 'em," said Jesse. "There's no way I'm going out with those things three times."

"No," Peter agreed. "But if there are a lot left over, maybe some of us can try selling them outside the grocery stores after school. We'll just have to see how many there are."

"Either way, St. Patrick's Day ought to be our last shot with these suckers," Jesse insisted. "Either we sell them or we don't. There comes a time when you just have to cut your losses and move on."

"I agree," Melanie said slowly, giving Jesse a strange look.

The rest of the group agreed too, and it was further decided that Leah would ask the principal for permission to sell the suckers at school. The meeting broke up with everyone in good spirits, optimistic about Eight Prime's chances of finally unloading the dreaded green suckers and making some money for the Junior Explorers.

Peter gathered up his photos as people began to leave, glad to hear them so positive. In his mind, though, he was already leaping ahead to the next fund-raiser. To go through with the day camp, he'd need money for bus maintenance, insurance, gas, and supplies—and that was on top of what it would take to fix up the campground.

Even the most wildly successful sucker sale would make just a drop in the bucket.

Four

"Hey, you're supposed to wrap that stuff around the stick, not your fingers," Leah teased. "It's going to get a lot harder when you can't move your hands anymore."

Jenna stifled her giggle quickly, clapping a hand over her mouth even though there were few people left to disturb in the library that afternoon. As usual on a Friday, most had fled the moment the last bell had rung, leaving Leah and Jenna a big back table to themselves. Untangling the roll of sticky green florist's tape from her hand, Jenna put it and the sucker it trailed from on the tabletop. "I don't think I'm going to be too great at this either way. Maybe you should do this part."

"If that's our best plan, we're in a lot of trouble," Leah said, holding up her own first attempt at taping. Jenna took one look and both girls burst out laughing.

"Whose idea was this again?" Leah asked between stifled peals.

"Gee, I wonder," Jenna gasped out.

Eventually they settled down enough to try again. Each girl had a roll of the tape that Leah's mom had donated to the cause, and Jenna had brought four rolls of narrow ribbon, two green and two white. A pair of scissors lay on the table, ready to cut off bow-length strips—if they ever got that far.

"My mom said to stretch the tape while you roll the stick underneath it. Move the sucker, not the tape." Feeling all thumbs, Leah did her best to follow her own advice. Her mom had demonstrated on a ballpoint pen at home, but the sucker stick was thinner and harder to work with. "There. That's better."

Cutting equal lengths of green and white ribbon, Jenna tied a two-tone bow at the base of the round green sucker, then held her creation against her lapel. "What do you think?" she asked, gesturing like a goofy game-show hostess.

"I think we have a winner. Only four hundred and ninety-nine more to go."

"Not quite. We sold something like forty on Valentine's Day."

"Wow, that's a load off my mind. Thank you, Ben!"

The girls giggled some more before settling down to work, gradually getting the hang of it. They had started out by agreeing to tape all the suckers, not just the ones for the guys, so there was plenty for them to do. Slowly the pile of green-stemmed suckers grew, and slowly Jenna grew silent. Her fingers wrapped faster and faster, but her brain seemed less involved.

It had been the same at the Eight Prime meeting the night before, Leah recalled. Jenna had taken the notes, as usual, but without her normal enthusiasm. She had been quick to offer to help with the suckers, but aside from that Leah could barely remember her speaking.

Not even to Peter.

The thought came like a revelation. Something was definitely bothering Jenna, and maybe it had nothing at all to do with Sarah. Maybe the problem was someone else.

Leah studied her friend from across the table. Jenna's eyes stayed on her work, but there was something different about them, something sad . . .

"Is something wrong, Jenna?" Leah heard herself asking. "Did you and Peter have a fight?"

Jenna looked up, startled.

"I'm sorry," Leah said hastily. "I don't mean to pry. It's just that you seem so down lately. If there's anything I can do . . ."

To Leah's surprise, Jenna's eyes filled with tears. "No, there's nothing. I wish!"

"But what's the matter, Jenna? Please tell me. I really want to help."

46

"It *is* Peter," Jenna admitted, her eyes flowing over. "But it's just stupid. I . . . I found out he kissed Melanie."

"Melanie *Andrews?*" As if there were any other. "*Peter* did? How did you find out?"

"He told me," Jenna said miserably, dragging a sleeve across her wet eyes.

"I can't believe it! Is he stupid?"

Jenna sniffed loudly. "That's one possible explanation."

"I—I—I just don't know what's worse," Leah sputtered. "That he did it, or that he told you about it."

"What's worst is having to relive it every time I see Melanie I can barely look at her."

"You poor thing." As if in a video replay, Leah remembered Melanie offering to help with the suckers, and Jenna quickly declining. No wonder she didn't want Melanie's help!

"I just can't believe Peter would cheat. He doesn't seem like the type." In fact, if Peter would cheat, who was safe? For that matter, what was Melanie thinking? Leah's mind was reeling.

Jenna had found a tissue somewhere. She wiped her face, then blew her nose. "He didn't cheat. Not really."

"Huh?" Leah's face had to have shown how confused she was.

"It happened in October, when we weren't to-gether yet. At the time we were even kind of fighting about—well . . . nothing really. But I just found out on Valentine's Day, and it's kind of hard to take. I don't know what to do, or how to act. It's making me crazy."

"Uh-huh." Leah rubbed her forehead, completely at a loss. If the kiss had happened before Peter and Jenna were a couple . . .

Still. Did he have to kiss Melanie? If Miguel ever kissed one of my friends . . .

"You can't tell anyone. Not even Miguel," Jenna said as if following her thoughts.

"But—"

Jenna shook her head. "Please, Leah. I don't want people to know. It's too embarrassing."

"But—"

"I'm glad I told you, though," she said with a sigh. "Not even my sisters know. And it's hard, keeping something like that to yourself."

Tell me about it!

Leah tried to smile reassuringly, but inside she was going nuts. She had promised herself she'd never keep secrets from Miguel again, but now what else could she do?

And what a secret, too!

I almost wish I'd never asked.

Melanie turned precisely on the last note of the music, hitting her final pose like a robot. Beaming her biggest, fakest smile, she wondered if her desperation was showing. It was practically dinnertime, and the whole squad was still at practice.

I thought cheerleading was supposed to be almost over! Instead, Sandra was working them harder than ever, determined to have perfection for the first open practice the next day. Melanie held her breath for the verdict.

"All right," Sandra said reluctantly. "I guess that's going to have to do it. I'll see you all bright and early tomorrow morning."

No one even dared to groan.

"And be sure to dress sharp—in school colors." Their coach checked her clipboard one last time, then walked off toward an exit.

"Man, what a workout," Tanya muttered as she and Melanie collected their things to leave. "I'm about to pass out from hunger."

"If I don't die of thirst first." Melanie tucked a sweaty towel into her gym bag and pulled out a bottle of water. "I've never seen Sandra so obsessive."

"Well, it's her first tryouts." Tanya glanced around, then lowered her voice. "She probably just wants to make sure she doesn't get another Vanessa."

Melanie laughed. "If that's her goal, then I'm behind her."

"Hey, you want a ride home? We could stop for something to eat on the way."

Melanie glanced at the caged clock high on the

gymnasium wall. Once again, there was no chance of reaching city hall before it closed.

"All right. Thanks," she said, trying to disguise her sigh. Every afternoon that week there had been something to keep her from trying to find the truth about her mother and Trent Wheeler. And the way things were going, she could be tied up all next week, too.

"So where do you want to eat?" Tanya asked as the girls climbed into her car. "Should we get hamburgers, or tacos?"

"Either way. Whatever you want."

"If you're not in a hurry to get home, we could sit down somewhere and order a pizza."

Melanie was hungry, but with all the other things on her mind the pangs were more of an annoyance than something she cared about satisfying. "Pizza's fine too."

Tanya laughed as she pulled out of the parking lot. "You're too easy. Something else on your mind?"

"Um, no. Not really." Nothing she wanted to talk about, anyway.

"Well, if you don't have an opinion, let's go to Burger City. Pizza sounds good, but it will take a long time and I might as well get home. I have an English paper to work on, and if my mom wants to go out tonight, I can make big points by baby-sitting the twins." Tanya grinned. "You never know when you're going to need big points."

Melanie nodded vaguely, not too worried about her own point count. Her father was never on top of things enough to prevent her from doing what she wanted anyway.

And once I learn how to drive, things will really open up. She imagined all the places she could go once she had her license. Getting downtown after school would be easy. Even getting to Iowa would be easy.

If only she were the one taking the driving test that weekend instead of Ben! What did Ben need to drive for, anyway? Where did he have to go? It didn't even seem fair.

"Did you get your driver's license right when you turned sixteen?" Melanie asked Tanya.

"The same day. I couldn't wait."

"Yeah, me either."

"Do you have your permit yet? You're old enough for that."

"I know, but I don't see any point. It's not like my dad is going to drive around with me for the next few months. He won't even let me take driver's ed. After . . . well . . . what happened with my mom . . . "

Tanya nodded understandingly. "He's not too eager to have you behind your own wheel."

"Exactly."

"If I were you, I'd definitely start pushing to get my permit, then. He's going to have to take you down there for the written test, and you'll need your birth certificate and Social Security card, too. You might as well start bugging him early. You know, to get him used to the idea."

Melanie nodded. "You may have a point." Getting her father to the examiner's station for her license was sure to be like pulling teeth. The last thing she wanted was to be stalled for months *after* she turned sixteen. "I don't even know where my birth certificate is. I guess it might be in the safe."

"Yeah, mine was in a safe-deposit box too," Tanya said, misunderstanding. "Mom had to go get it at the bank, which meant she had to leave work to do it on a lunch hour, and . . ." Tanya rolled her eyes. "Just take my word for it. You're not going to believe how many excuses they can come up with."

She turned a corner, still shaking her head. "I don't even know why she had to lock it up in the first place. I mean, it's not like some dangerous criminal is going to break into our house and go straight for my birth certificate. But Mom keeps all our important papers at the bank, in case there's a fire or something."

"That's really kind of smart," Melanie said, but she was barely paying attention as her mind took off with a whole new idea.

Unlike Tanya's mom, the Andrewses didn't fool around with safe-deposit boxes. They had their own safe—a big one—cemented right into a wall of the house. Melanie remembered how, when she was a little girl, she had loved to follow her mother to the safe to try on something spectacular from her extensive jewelry collection. Her father had been in and out of the safe a lot in those days too, messing around with his stock certificates and pink slips on the classic cars her parents had collected.

Since her mother had died, though, Melanie had all but forgotten about the safe. She could remember her father getting into it once, right after the accident, to lock up the rest of her mother's jewelry. The pink slips would be gone now, because all but one of the cars had been sold, but there had been other papers too. The more Melanie thought about it, the more certain she became that her birth certificate would be there. Her parents' marriage license would be there.

And who knows what else I might find? she thought, heart fluttering with excitement.

There was only one problem: She didn't know the combination. Her parents had never allowed her to open the safe on her own.

Still, how hard can it be to guess? The combination on the storage room was the date of her mother's death. *The safe's probably their anniversary. Or somebody's birthday. I'll bet I can figure it out.*

Even if she couldn't, the combination had to be written down somewhere in her father's office. She ought to be able to find it. . . .

Melanie took a deep breath, full of her new plan. Now all she had to do was get him out of the house long enough to put it into action.

Miguel checked in for his third shift at the hospital, already feeling like a pro. In the nurses' lounge, he shed his coat and pulled his neatly folded scrub top on over his T-shirt, making sure his name tag was straight. Then, without asking anyone what to do, he grabbed the book he had left in his cubbyhole and headed straight for Zachary's room.

"Hey, how's that mac and cheese?" he asked, walking up to the bed.

Zach pulled a face from behind his dinner tray. "Yuck."

"It's not that bad, is it? You've got pudding."

"Hooray." Zach mustered a surprising amount of sarcasm for a nine-year-old. Putting down his fork, he turned his attention to Miguel. "You know what I really like? Kung pao chicken. Have you ever had that?"

"I . . . might have. I'm not sure. It's awfully spicy, isn't it?"

"I like spicy stuff," Zach said wistfully. "All they ever give me here is baby food."

"Well, it's just for a little while. You'll be out of here pretty soon, and then you can eat whatever you want."

Zach looked surprised, but before he could say anything, a tall, thin woman burst into the room, wearing a harried expression.

"How's my baby?" she asked, rushing forward and wrapping Zach in a hug. "I'm so sorry I'm late. I had to finish up something at work, but I got here as fast as I could."

"Hi, Mom," said Zach, looking slightly embarrassed. "That's okay."

"Hi. I'm Maxine Dewey," she said, holding out a hand to Miguel. "And you are . . . ?" She tilted her head to read his name tag. "Oh, Miguel! Zach told me about you. I really appreciate your reading to him in the afternoon, keeping him company. I hate it that I can't be here during the day, but Zach and I are alone now, and if I don't keep my job . . ."

Moving closer to the bed, she put a hand on Zach's forehead, then ran her fingers back through his tufted hair.

"That's all you're going to eat?" she asked, nodding toward his nearly full tray. "I don't think so."

"Mommm!" Zach shot Miguel a mortified look.

"Your mom's right," said Miguel, feeling suddenly extraneous. "And since she's here to keep you

55

company now, I think I'd better go and hang out with some other kid."

"What about our story?" Zach whined. "I want to know what happens!"

"I'll leave the book here," said Miguel, placing it on the end of the bed. "Maybe you can read to your mom tonight."

"Thank you." Mrs. Dewey flashed him a smile.

"I'll see you tomorrow, buddy," said Miguel, waving as he left. "We'll pick up wherever you leave off."

Miguel had barely stepped into the hall when he spotted Dr. Wells coming out of the room two doors down. The pair had eventually met on Miguel's first day at the hospital, but Miguel hadn't seen the man since. Dr. Wells had explained then that he worked varying hours, and it would be up to Miguel to coordinate with the nurses to find ways to make himself useful. The doctor would keep tabs on him through nurse reports, a weekly time sheet, and occasional meetings.

"Hey! How are you doing, Miguel?" Dr. Wells greeted him. "Keeping busy?"

"Trying. I was going to read to Zach, but his mom's here now, so I guess I'd better find someone else. I think I'll check out the playroom."

"Why don't you tag along with me on my rounds? It'll give you a chance to see what I do here."

"Great!" Miguel said eagerly.

The first room they visited belonged to five-year-old Lucy Small.

"How's Miss Lucy?" Dr. Wells asked, making a mock-serious face. "Do you have a minute to listen to my heart?"

The little girl giggled. "Again?"

Miguel watched as Dr. Wells checked her over, letting her listen to his heart through the stethoscope before he applied it to her.

"Can you take a really, really deep breath?" he asked. "Pretend you're going to scream, only don't."

Lucy sucked in the required breath, trying to hold it against her giggles.

"Well, you are doing just fantastic!" the doctor proclaimed. "I think you'd better have some ice cream tonight to celebrate."

"Can I?"

"You bet. We'll send Miguel here down to the kitchen a little later."

Out in the hall, Dr. Wells smiled as he made some notes. "Lucy came in with a burst appendix. We took care of that and then she caught pneumonia. It was scary for a while, but her lungs sound much better now. She'll be out in a few more days."

The preteen boy in the next room had broken both his femurs in a motorbike accident. Now two long casts kept him flat on his back.

"How are the legs, Chuck?" Dr. Wells asked. "Are you hurting anywhere?"

Chuck shook his head. "Not really, but it's so uncomfortable just lying here like this. When are you going to let me get up?"

"Pretty soon."

Dr. Wells checked Chuck's chart, then sat in the chair beside the bed. "The good news is that you'll be able to walk, probably even play sports, so try to focus on that."

Chuck managed a smile. "I do. It's all I think about."

"Not to mention that soon you'll be the Nintendo champion of Clearwater Crossing," the doctor teased, pointing at the kid's Game Boy. "If you get bored with that, though, Miguel here could find you some books, or a puzzle, or stuff to draw with. Rumor has it he can even talk the kitchen out of ice cream."

"I don't know how that rumor got started," Miguel said uneasily, afraid he wouldn't be able to deliver.

Dr. Wells winked. "I'll give them a call."

Back in the hallway, the doctor shook his head. "I can't believe a kid that age was jumping motorcycles," he told Miguel in a low voice. "I know other people do it, but if you'd seen the damage on that one . . . Chuck and his parents are both really lucky he didn't bleed to death."

Miguel nodded, then blurted out the questions

58

he'd been dying to ask for three days. "What's wrong with Zach Dewey? Why is he in here?"

Dr. Wells looked surprised. "You don't know?"

"Nobody told me, and I didn't want to pry. If it's okay, though, I'd really like to know."

"Zach has Wilms' tumor, a type of kidney cancer. He's in for chemo to shrink the mass before it's removed in surgery."

"Cancer?" Miguel gasped. "But Zach's so young!"

"This type of cancer strikes young, and normally, when it gets caught early, you take out the affected kidney, do a little chemotherapy, and that's the end of it. Unfortunately, in Zach's case the tumor is very large, with metastases on the lungs. The tumor thrombus has extended into the right atrium, too, which makes removing it considerably more dangerous."

"But . . ." Miguel felt everything stop for a moment. The bright hallway in front of him seemed to grow dim. "He's going to make it, right? I mean, he's not going to die."

Dr. Wells smiled reassuringly. "Not if I have anything to do with it. I won't say his case isn't more serious than most, but once the tumor responds to treatment it should be a straightforward surgery. After that, more chemo and radiation, but there's good news, too. Zach's tumor has what we call a favorable histology. The vast majority of kids survive this."

"Thank God," said Miguel, his voice shaking with relief.

"So how many hours are you working?" Dr. Wells asked. "Are you keeping a time sheet, like we discussed?"

Miguel nodded. "I've been coming in as much as I can, but I could try to do more if you want."

"Actually, I was going to say you can come in less. I know you must have homework, and other obligations for school."

True, thought Miguel. But working for Sabrina had conditioned him to do his homework late at night, and he really wanted to spend as many hours at the hospital as they'd let him.

What am I going to do next week, though, when water polo practice starts?

In an instant, he knew the answer. *I won't be on the team.*

It didn't even feel like a sacrifice anymore, and he wasn't doing it for the money, either. Being at the hospital was just more interesting—not to mention more important. Helping kids like Zach was worth any price.

I'll tell Coach K. on Monday.

Miguel wasn't looking forward to that encounter any more than he had relished quitting his job with Mr. Ambrosi, but at the same time he knew he wouldn't change his mind. In fact, just making the decision was an unexpected relief. It seemed he had spent half his life watching other people chase their dreams. Now, at last, he had one of his own.

"Don't you worry about me," he told Dr. Wells. "At this point I'd probably be here even if I had to pay you."

Five

"All right. That's the dance," Vanessa Winters told the crowd of cheerleading contestants as the current squad hit its last pose. Stooping beside the boom box on the gym floor, she pushed the Stop button. "We perform it in formation, but for tryouts you'll all learn it the same way."

Sandra stepped in front of Vanessa to address the girls in the bleachers. "According to the sign-up sheet, there are ninety-six girls here today. Everyone, please come down to the floor and split into groups of twelve."

There was a rumble of confusion as the candidates drained out of the bleachers, self-consciously joining the cheerleaders on the basketball court. Nicole picked her way carefully along the benches, praying she wouldn't trip or do anything ungraceful. The bright white athletic shoes on her feet were brand-new, setting off the fresh bottled tan on her legs. She had spent hours at the mall the afternoon before putting together the perfect first-practice outfit: green shorts, a gold sports top, and a hooded white sweatshirt.

Now, looking around at the other girls there that Saturday morning, Nicole was satisfied with her choices, not to mention the extra flair she'd given her hairstyle and makeup. Even compared to the prettier girls, she looked like a contender, and most of the real cheerleaders were dressed a lot like she was. *This could be the year*, she thought hopefully, joining the crowd on the floor.

Sandra clapped her hands to be heard above the noise. "It doesn't matter how you split up, just do it quickly," she called. "Eight groups of twelve—let's go!"

Nicole hurriedly joined the nearest cluster of girls, trying to look as if they were lucky to get her. They all smiled a little—tight, nervous smiles—but no one spoke. Instead they stood there sizing one another up until Sandra walked over.

"How many have we got here?" she asked, counting. "Ten? We need two more. You, and you." Pointing to a couple of girls still on the fringes, Sandra motioned them over. "Tiffany!" she called. "You take this group."

Sandra moved on, checking the other groups and assigning them leaders, while Tiffany Barrett sauntered over to the one Nicole was in.

"I'm Tiffany," she said smugly. "But of course you already know that. We'll go there."

Pointing to a corner, Tiffany led the way, a boom box dangling from red-tipped fingers. Unlike her squadmates, she wore a plain white tank top with her cheerleading skirt, making Nicole almost desperate with envy.

"Okay," she said, turning to face her group. "Let's get to it. The way we learn a new dance is by breaking it down into counts of eight. We'll start with four or five eights, and when you guys can keep up with my count you can try it to the music.

"Well?" Tiffany's hands went to her hips. "Line up or something."

The girls shuffled around nervously, not sure how many lines to make, or who should be in each. Eventually they settled on two lines of six, Nicole snagging a place front and center.

After all, tryouts really start now, she thought. Sure, the auditions were important, but Nicole was certain the contestants were already being watched every minute. It could only help her case to show her leadership qualities early.

"We need to straighten up," she announced, holding out her arms to align the girls on either side of her. They looked at her strangely but followed along.

A minute later, however, Nicole wished she had waited a little longer before making herself stand out.

"Here's the first eight," said Tiffany, moving her

body as she counted. "*One*, two, *three*, four, *five*, six, *seven*, eight. Got it? One more time: *One*, two, *three*, four, *five*, six, *seven*, eight. Okay, let's see it."

Tiffany stopped demonstrating and began counting again, as if she actually expected them to do the first part of the dance after only those two brief glimpses. Then, to Nicole's amazement, half the girls in her group actually did.

"What about the rest of you?" Tiffany asked. "Are you planning to stand there all day? *One*, two, *three*, four, *five*, six, *seven*, eight."

Panicked, Nicole stumbled awkwardly through the steps, doing her best to copy the other girls. Right hand—no—*left* hand on hip and turn and turn and kick, sidestep left. Was that it? No, turn the other way. The *other* foot!

"All right. Second eight." Without pausing even a second, Tiffany began counting out the next moves.

The following half hour was a nightmare as Nicole tried desperately to keep up, feeling like the most uncoordinated dork in the gym.

I didn't have this much trouble last year! So why was she tied up in her own legs now, like a spider playing Twister?

It only got worse when Tiffany turned on the music. No one could possibly be expected to remember so much so quickly, not to mention that the music was twice as fast as Tiffany had been counting.

Nicole was convinced she had never looked more pathetic as she staggered along with the others, stumbling all over herself.

Then came the cheer. In addition to learning a completely new set of steps, now they were supposed to remember a bunch of random phrases and shout them at the same time.

"Go green. Go gold," she shouted desperately, clapping out of synch. "Be . . ."

Ugh! she groaned to herself. *What were they supposed to be again?*

The other shouts echoing through the gym only confused her further, until she could barely think.

"Add chewing gum to this, and that blonde is out of here," Nicole heard someone behind her crack, to appreciative snickering.

By the time the humiliating session finally came to an end, Nicole would have given anything for a great big rock to crawl under. Tiffany was staring as if Nicole had just landed from Planet Futile, and the other girls wouldn't even look at her. Running for her backpack, Nicole prepared to flee out a side door.

And then she changed her mind. If she wasn't prepared to give up altogether, she shouldn't be seen slinking out with her tail between her legs. Not on the first day.

Catching sight of Melanie talking to Tanya and Angela, Nicole hurried over to the other side of the gym instead. Maybe she could make up some of the good-impression points she'd just lost with Tiffany by schmoozing Melanie and her friends. *After all, Tiffany's graduating, but those guys will still be around.*

"Hi, Melanie," she said loudly, breaking into the conversation. "Pretty good practice today, huh?"

Melanie rolled her eyes. "Oh, yeah. I can't think of anything I'd rather do on a Saturday morning."

Angela and Tanya laughed.

"Which reminds me," Melanie added with a sideways glance at the clock, "I really need to get out of here now."

"You want a ride home?" Nicole asked quickly.

"Tanya's taking me. See ya, Nicole."

Melanie and Tanya walked off one way and Angela went the other. Nicole was left by herself again, feeling like even more of an idiot than before. All three cheerleaders had virtually ignored her.

Had anyone else noticed?

She glanced fearfully around the gym, but luckily the building had almost emptied. With as much dignity as she could muster, Nicole hurried out the nearest door and ran for the parking lot.

Maybe Guy will call me tonight, she thought hopefully as she climbed into the car. *He always makes me feel better.*

I hope Courtney doesn't call me. She was already feeling insecure enough without being ridiculed by her best friend.

The only reason I was so clumsy today was because I was so nervous, she reassured herself. *Not that Court's likely to see it that way.*

No, Courtney was certain to make a hundred sarcastic remarks—assuming she was finally ready to talk about something other than Jeff.

Jeff was the last thing Nicole wanted to talk about, and not just because she had other things on her mind, either. There simply wasn't anything good that could come from covering that ground again.

Because, sooner or later, Courtney is bound to blame me for that mess.

"You're *sure* you want to go through with this?" Mr. Pipkin repeated.

"Yes, Dad," Ben said impatiently. "Would you please stop asking me that? You're not exactly helping my confidence."

From his position behind the wheel, Ben shot an injured look at his father, who was standing on the pavement next to the driver's side of the car. Then he glanced nervously back in the other direction, at the examination station. His driving examiner would walk out through that door any minute, and Ben's driving test would begin.

Might as well use the time to review, Ben told himself, trying to stay calm. *Do the parts of the car. Okay. Parking brake, accelerator, brake pedal. Right turn signal, left turn signal, headli—*

No! Water squirted onto the windshield, spraying Mr. Pipkin in the process.

"Those are the windshield wipers," Mr. Pipkin said through gritted teeth. Removing his water-spotted glasses, he wiped them on the inside of his shirt.

"I know that. I just, uh, didn't know they were going to squirt *you*."

Ben used the rubber blades to swipe off the glass just as a formidable-looking woman approached the car, making a slow circuit to check all four tires and the license plate. She wore navy-blue pants with an immaculately ironed blue shirt, and the bun on top of her head looked like a half-scoop of steel ice cream.

"Horn," she demanded, stopping outside Ben's open window. A name tag pinned to her shirt identified her as SMITH.

Oh please, please do it right, he thought as he reached for the horn. He couldn't possibly confuse *that* with the windshield wipers. Could he?

The horn blared—a deep, rich tone—and Ben breathed a sigh of relief.

Smith marked something on her clipboard, then proceeded around to the passenger side, where she opened the door and inspected the seat belt. "You are supposed to provide a *clean* seat for the examiner," she told him.

"It, uh, is," Ben said nervously. "I was just sitting in it myself."

Her eyes were the same shade of gray as her hair. Narrowing them slightly, she reached into the crack of the seat and extracted something with two unpolished fingertips—an ancient, flattened gum wrapper. "Then this must be yours," she said, handing it over with distaste.

Ben shoved the paper into the ashtray, turning to look for help from his father, but Mr. Pipkin had withdrawn to wait beside the building. *This is the real deal*, Ben realized. *I'm taking this test for better or worse.*

And it had already started.

Smith buckled herself into the passenger seat and checked the parking brake suspiciously, as if to make certain she'd be able to slow them down at the point in the near future when Ben was sure to endanger their lives. Then she began running him through the checklist, marking off the items as he found them.

"Turn signal . . . accelerator . . . foot brake . . . parking brake . . . windshield wipers . . . Wrong. Those are the headlights."

Ben's eyes widened with horror; his heart leapt into his throat. Had he actually just *done* that? How *could* he?

"No! I know where the windshield wipers are!" he bleated desperately. "Believe me, I use them all the time!" His hands shook almost uncontrollably as he demonstrated spraying and wiping the wind-

70

shield, but Smith was already writing something on her sheet.

"What are you doing?" he asked, leaning over to look. "You're not going to take points off for that?"

"Do not speak to the examiner unless it's urgent," Smith said, shielding the clipboard against her chest. "You may start the vehicle and pull onto the street, proceeding forward. I will tell you where to turn."

The keys jangled in his hand as Ben turned them in the ignition. Luckily his father's car was an automatic and easy to start. Releasing the parking brake, he put the car in gear and crept out onto the road.

Smith began writing again.

"What?" Ben asked hysterically.

"You didn't check to see if the way was clear and—"

"But you told me to go!"

"*And* you didn't signal."

"Signal to who? There was nobody there!"

Smith was still writing, unmoved. "How would you know? You never looked." She raised her eyes from her clipboard. "Are you driving or rolling? What is the speed limit here?"

"Um . . . uh . . ." Ben looked frantically for a sign. He couldn't find one, but there was a house up ahead. "Twenty-five!" he cried. "Twenty-five in a residential zone!"

"Nice try. But this is a mixed-use zone with a posted speed of thirty-five. There was a big fat sign in front of you the whole time you waited for me." Smith went for her clipboard again.

"But . . . but . . ." Ben felt as if he were one red mark short of bursting into tears. He wanted to argue his case, to plead that she wasn't being fair. But one look at his examiner's unyielding profile convinced him that arguing would only seal his fate. He didn't even know how many points he had already lost. Besides, she had told him not to talk to her.

"Do I still have any chance of passing?" he blurted out. "I have to know. Because I *have* to pass."

"Don't think I haven't heard that before. You kids always have to pass. Anyone would think it was life and death."

"It is! If you knew how much grief people will . . . I'll *die* if I don't pass this test."

Smith's gray eyebrows raised just a fraction before a slow, wicked smile found her lips. "In that case, Mr. Pipkin, why don't we change the order of things a bit and proceed directly to parallel parking? That could put us both out of our misery a lot quicker."

Oh, great, thought Miguel.

Sabrina had just passed his pew to join the communion line.

72

What's she doing at this mass? I thought she went Saturday nights now.

Miguel, his mother, and his younger sister, Rosa, had been attending the late-morning Sunday mass for a while, but he'd only ever seen Sabrina there once. He watched as she received communion with the rest of the back-pew occupants, then began strolling back up the aisle to her seat. Miguel and his family were only a few pews from the front; she'd be passing them in a second.

I don't want to talk to her. Not today.

He watched with trepidation, ready to avert his glance the moment she looked his way. But she never did. Continuing with meekly lowered eyes, she walked right by the del Rioses as if she didn't even know they were there.

Maybe she doesn't, he thought hopefully.

But his hopes were dashed the moment his family left the church. Sabrina was waiting for him outside on the steps, looking amazing in a new lilac coat and matching pants, silver bangles on both wrists.

"Can I talk to you a minute? Alone?" Her voice was low and urgent, her violet eyes pleading.

"Sabrina! How are you, dear?" Mrs. del Rios cried, clearly delighted to run into the daughter of her old friend.

"We haven't seen you for a while," Rosa said happily. "Are you coming over for lunch?"

Miguel cringed. That was *all* he needed.

"Thanks, but I can't," Sabrina said quickly. Her hand brushed his arm, the lightest of touches. "Miguel?"

"I, uh . . . I'm—"

"It'll only take a minute. You don't mind if I borrow Miguel a sec, do you?" Sabrina flashed his mother a brilliant smile. "We'll hurry."

"Take your time, dear. I want to talk to Father Sebastian anyway."

"I'll meet you at the car in two minutes," Miguel called loudly as Sabrina pulled him around the side of the building.

At least we're still at church, he thought, shrugging off Sabrina's hand but following behind her. *How much trouble can we get into here?*

She stopped at last beside the tall marble statue at the center of the courtyard. The church garden stretched around them, empty and cold. They were alone.

"What do you want, Sabrina?" he asked. His voice had an edge that he hadn't intended, but the thought of the disastrous last time he'd seen her was still fresh in his mind. *Too fresh.*

"You're mad. I was afraid you would be."

Miguel closed his eyes, shutting out the courtyard. "I'm not mad," he said with a sigh. "But you did take me by surprise. I wish . . . well . . . I just feel weird about everything now, and—"

74

"I know." Sabrina cut him off with a catch in her voice. "I know, and I am so, so sorry. That's what I wanted to say. I want to apologize."

Miguel's eyes snapped open. "You do?"

"Of course." Sabrina's gaze was on her feet. Her shiny black hair fell like a veil across her pretty face. "You have no idea how embarrassed I am. I feel like such an idiot."

What a relief! Not that he wanted her to feel like an idiot . . .

Miguel stretched a comforting hand toward her head, then abruptly drew it back. *Maybe that's not such a good idea.*

"Let's just forget about it," he urged. "I will if you will."

Sabrina was almost in tears. "I just felt like I was losing you," she said miserably. "Like if I didn't act fast you'd be gone. I . . . I don't know what got into me. Of course you could never be interested in me."

"What? Why not?" *Oh, no. Did I just say that?* "I mean, it's not you, Sabrina. I think you're great." *Not to mention too gorgeous for words.* "It's just that I already have a girlfriend," he said firmly.

She looked up at him through wet black lashes. "So if you didn't . . . I mean, if it weren't for Leah . . . I'd have a chance?"

A chance? He'd have had her in his arms five minutes ago.

75

"Well, I . . . uh . . . It's just . . . I really don't think we should. . . . There *is* a Leah."

Sabrina nodded. "You're right. I only wanted you to know that I'm sorry—and that you don't have to worry. I'll never do anything like that again."

She hesitated, then reached for one of his hands, enclosing it in both of her own. Her eyes searched his as if trying to read his soul. "But if you ever want to call me . . . I mean, ever. Anytime. Well, you know where I am."

With just a hint of a smile, she dropped his hand and walked away, leaving him reeling behind her.

That was an apology? It had sounded more like an invitation.

I do *know where you are*, he thought, breathing in the perfume she'd left on his fingers. *I really wish I didn't.*

Six

"So you passed. Congratulations," Mark Foster said. "What score did you get?"

Ben's proud smile dimmed just a shade as he glanced around the packed computer lab. "I don't remember. I'm not sure they even told me."

Mark's face showed his disbelief. "Of course they told you. They have to tell you."

"Well, uh . . . ," Ben stalled, trying to think of a good reply. He didn't want to lie, but no way could he tell his friend he had passed by only one point. That was almost as bad as failing. Every time Ben remembered the trauma of taking his driving test, parallel parking under Smith's eagle eye . . .

"Look, there's Angela!" he said gratefully, stifling a shudder.

The cheerleader had just walked into the lab with a girl Ben didn't know. The two of them approached the front counter to be assigned a computer, but before they could speak Ben was at their side.

"Hi!" he greeted Angela. "Guess what! I got my driver's license last weekend."

The other girl snickered. But Angela smiled.

"Congratulations," she said with a wink. "Now your dating days begin in earnest."

She and her friend turned and started talking to the teacher behind the counter before Ben could collect his wits. Was she teasing? Or was she *flirting*? Ben spun on his heel and ran back to Mark.

"Did you hear that? Angela said now that I have my license I can start some serious dating."

"Ah. A comedian," Mark said wryly. Since his track record with girls wasn't any better than Ben's, he could make a comment like that. This time, however, Ben wasn't listening.

"No, Mark. She *winked* at me when she said it. Like . . . I don't know . . . ." His heart was hammering so hard he could barely think. "Like, well . . . do you think she might have been hinting?"

Mark's jaw dropped. Then he threw back his head and laughed. "Hinting that she wants to go out with *you*?" he hooted, beside himself. "Yeah, sure. Dream on!"

"Keep it down," Ben begged, cringing as he glanced around the lab. He couldn't blame Mark for his reaction, though. He felt kind of stupid now for even mentioning something so unlikely.

Except that sometimes long shots came through. And if there was any chance that Angela would go out with him—any chance at all—wouldn't he be even more stupid not to take it?

After all, miracles do *happen*, he thought, gazing longingly in the direction she had gone.

So people said, anyway. Ben had never experienced one personally.

There's a first time for everything, he reminded himself, returning to the computer program he and Mark were creating.

But even that wasn't really true. There were plenty of firsts he had yet to experience, and a whole bunch more he was sure he never would: first ten million dollars, first marriage to a supermodel, first house in the Bahamas, first day in high school being treated like a stud . . .

Ben sighed. *Earning the ten million dollars is more likely than that.*

Still . . . she *had* winked at him.

What did he really have to lose?

Peter's stomach was tied in knots by the time he and Chris pulled into the lake parking lot Monday afternoon. He had barely been able to concentrate on his classes, and now that he was finally about to meet with a ranger he felt more nervous still.

"I don't know, Peter," Chris said dubiously. "The place looks pretty deserted."

"That has to be his truck," Peter said, pointing. "I'll bet he walked out to the Boy Scouts' camp."

They hurried down the trail, Peter leading the way. The sky overhead was leaden gray, threatening to drop more snow onto the path, but Peter crunched through the thin, icy patches already there almost without noticing.

"If it were any warmer, this trail would be solid mud," Chris observed from behind him.

"Yeah, but it will dry out by summer."

"Sure. It never rains in the summer."

Peter glanced back over his shoulder, only to find Chris smiling, pleased with his little joke. "Chris! Don't you start too."

"I'm just giving you a hard time."

"Who isn't?"

"What?"

"Never mind."

Peter had spotted the ranger up ahead. The man was standing at the water's edge by the rotted remains of the dock. Hands in his jacket pockets, he huddled down into his collar, gazing across the lake. Forgetting everything else, Peter ran to join him.

"Hi!" he called as he closed the last few feet between them. "Hi, I'm Peter. I hope you haven't been waiting long—I just got out of school."

The man shook his head and held out a hand. "Nah, I came a little early on purpose, to take a look around. I'm Bud Williams."

"Nice to meet you."

Chris stepped in to shake hands as well. "Chris Hobart."

"Well, it certainly looks like you boys have your work cut out for you," Bud said, gesturing with one arm. "This place is a mess. Probably take you a couple of days just to rake it out. As far as the dock goes . . ." He shook his head. "Maybe you can save those supports, maybe not. They look pretty rotten, but I'm not going to wade out there to check."

Chris laughed. "Me either."

"If we can save them, we'll probably build a new dock. If not, we'll pull out the rotten wood to make the lake safer for swimmers," Peter told the ranger, hoping he sounded confident and mature. "We'll put new windows on the shed and paint it. We'll bring in a couple of portable outhouses for toilets, and there's supposed to be a water line out here somewhere. I'd like to tap into that for a sink and drinking fountain."

Bud nodded. "I found the pipe before you got here. It stubs out next to that big oak."

Peter followed the man's finger. The tree Bud pointed to was near the center of the level clearing, whereas the shed was off to one side. "That's kind of in the middle of nowhere, isn't it?"

"It is now. I think there used to be another building there."

"That's no big deal," Chris said. "We'll just build a box around an upright pipe, with the drinking fountain on top and the sink attached to one side. We'd better add a hose spigot while we're at it."

"Good idea," said Bud. "That ought to cover all the bases."

"If we can, I'd like to build some picnic tables, too. If we can afford it, I mean." Peter took a deep breath, almost afraid to ask the next question. "So can we have the place? For a dollar a day?"

Bud nodded. "As long as there's an adult on-site the whole time your camp is in session." He turned to Chris. "You twenty-one, son?"

"I will be, but I can't be around that much. Peter and I have been taking care of these kids for the last two years, though. He knows them well, and he's very responsible."

"Even so. Things happen. People get hurt." Bud shook his head. "You need an adult out here. And a telephone, too."

"But . . ." Peter had hoped his past experience would deflect the age issue, especially since Chris would still be around sometimes. Where was he going to get an adult for the whole summer?

"If I find a full-time adult and get a phone, then do we have a deal? A dollar a day?"

Bud laughed. "Yes, a dollar a day. You sure do know how to stick to a point, son. You get an adult on the project and you've got a deal."

They shook on the agreement, Peter wondering how he was going to come through on his end, but by the time he and Chris had hiked back to the parking lot, he had already solved half the problem.

"We can get a cell phone," he said as they climbed into his old Toyota. "That's no big deal."

"Nope. Just more money."

Peter started the car and headed for town. "And Bud never said it had to be the *same* adult here all those hours. If my mom would come one day a week, and maybe Jenna's mom, or some of the older, retired people at church . . . I could have a whole volunteer schedule."

Chris nodded amiably. "Some of them might even think it was fun."

"It *is* going to be fun. I wish you were going to be there."

"Yeah. But it's not like I'm disappearing. I'll stop by once in a while to—"

"What?" Peter prompted, not liking the way his friend had stopped in the middle of a sentence.

Chris's eyes squeezed shut, as if he had developed a sudden headache.

"What, Chris?"

"Have you, uh . . . have you considered who's going to drive the bus?"

"Oh, no! The bus!" Peter groaned, slapping his forehead. "How could I have missed something so obvious?"

Because of the number of passengers, the bus driver had to have a commercial license. And in order to get that license, a person had to be eighteen. No one in Eight Prime was old enough to qualify, which was why Chris had been their driver from the start.

"Well, summer's a long way off. We'll figure something out," Chris said.

"How?"

"Why not look on the bright side? You found a camp, and it's a pretty good one, too. By the time it's all fixed up, you'll be styling. You know what you ought to do? Put a flagpole up by the shed. Then you can fly the American flag and have a camp flag, too."

Peter could already see them, waving in a warm June breeze. "That would be cool."

Could my mom make us a camp flag? Or should I let Eight Prime design it? They might feel more a part of things if they did. Maybe they could hold an Eight Prime meeting at the lake, too, so everyone could see things for themselves. If the whole group got behind him . . .

I still won't *have a driver.*

Peter drew a deep breath, then shrugged. The bus thing would work itself out.

"Oh, come on," Melanie muttered under her breath. "What else could it be?"

She glanced nervously over her shoulder, relieved to see the library doorway still empty. Her father was asleep downstairs in the den and, even though it was a huge risk messing with the safe while he was in the house, this was the first good opportunity she'd had.

Except that for all the progress I'm making, I might as well not have tried.

She had entered the library soundlessly, laying a few books around in case she needed a cover story. Then, holding her breath against the slightest noise, she had managed to remove the false cabinet panel concealing the safe's door and its combination dial—a dial that was now growing slick with Melanie's nervous sweat.

Come on, Melanie. Think!

She had already tried every combination she could guess. Her parents' wedding anniversary had been her first try, followed by her mother's birthday, her father's, then her own. She didn't think it would be the anniversary of her mother's death—the safe had been installed long before that, and besides, that was the combination for the storage room. Now she spun out those numbers anyway, her hand clumsy with agitation.

Nothing.

Maybe I'm not doing it right. Maybe I have to spin in the opposite direction. Or go around more times. Or start on zero. Or end on zero. Or . . . Why didn't I ever pay attention when my parents were doing this?

She started back through her guesses again, spinning in the opposite direction, but her nervousness increased with every turn. If her father caught her sneaking around with the safe, he'd know she was up to no good.

"If you wanted something in there, why didn't you ask me?" she could practically hear him demanding.

But she didn't *want* to ask him. Not while there was still a way in the world to avoid it. And she definitely didn't want to tell him what it was she was after.

The last birthday combination failed again. *This is hopeless! I could be here until Christmas at this rate.*

Not to mention that her nerves were totally shot. With shaking hands, she fitted the false panel back on the cabinet. She breathed a little easier when it clicked into place, eliminating the chance that she might be caught. Frustrated but not defeated, she began putting the books away.

I'll just have to find the combination, she thought. *Dad must have it written down somewhere, and I'll bet it's in his study.*

There was no chance of looking there now, though. Not with him passed out right across the hall.

I've had enough excitement for tonight anyway. Still moving like a thief, Melanie snuck down the hall to her bedroom, immensely relieved when the door closed securely behind her.

She'd waited this long to learn the truth. What was one more day?

Seven

"Are you going to see Zach today?" Leah asked. She and Miguel were hanging out beside his car in the student parking lot, savoring the last few moments before he left for Tuesday's shift.

"Of course. I promised to teach him chess."

"Isn't he kind of young for that?"

Miguel shook his head. "The younger he learns, the better he'll be. All the prodigies learn young—that's why they're called prodigies."

"I see. So now you're coaching the next Bobby Fischer."

"You never know," Miguel said happily. "I've got to go."

With a quick kiss good-bye, he climbed into his car. They both sighed with relief when its cranky old engine started.

"I'll call you tonight," he promised through the open window.

Leah bent down. "One more kiss."

Their lips met again, lingering this time. Leah's hand found the back of his head, pulling him closer.

She buried her fingers in his hair, trailing them down the warm skin of his neck. For a moment she forgot she was standing in a freezing parking lot, bent in a totally unnatural position. All she felt was the heat of skin on skin and the depth of their love for each other. His teeth caught her bottom lip, tugging gently before he let her go.

"I love you. But I really have to leave."

"Yeah, okay." Reluctantly, almost breathless, she stepped away from the car. As many times as she'd kissed Miguel, a kiss like that still made her heart race. "I love you too."

She waved as he drove off, and by the time she had let herself into her mother's car, Leah was already hatching a new idea.

I ought to plan something really romantic for this Friday night. Something special, to show Miguel how I feel.

Hearing about Jenna's problems with Peter had only reminded Leah how lucky she was that things were so good between her and Miguel now. It wasn't at all hard to imagine herself in the same position as Jenna—not with Sabrina Ambrosi working overtime to make something like that happen.

Leah pulled out of the parking lot. *I am so, so glad to be rid of her.*

Not only was Miguel safely at another job now, but she hadn't heard Sabrina's name once for an entire week. *What a welcome change!*

If Miguel ever cheated on her . . .

But he hasn't. And he's not going to, she told herself quickly, not even wanting to think about it.

This Friday night, I'm going to come up with a way to show him how much I appreciate his loyalty.

"Miguel! Where are you going?"

Miguel stopped and turned in the polished hallway. "Oh, hi, Howard. I was on my way to see Zach."

"I've got something else for you to do," the nurse said briskly. "Follow me."

"But—but," Miguel sputtered to Howard's back as they walked. "I promised Zach we'd play chess."

Howard led him into the nurses' lounge and closed the door behind them.

"Look, Miguel, I'm glad you're taking care of Zach. He's a nice kid, and I like him too. But you have to spread yourself around a little better. We're not supposed to have favorites."

"I know," Miguel said sheepishly. "But Zach and I have become friends."

"Go say hello to him for a minute, then, but I want you to hang out with someone else today. Preferably with a few different someones."

"Okay," Miguel said reluctantly, imagining how disappointed Zach was going to be.

"Listen, Miguel. These kids come through here, and some of them stay a long time. But the ones who are lucky leave and forget all about us. The best thing that could happen in Zach's case is that he'll get well, go home, and this will all shrink to an old memory. It's what we want, what we work for. If you're the praying type, you ought to be praying for that."

Miguel nodded, but it wasn't what he wanted to hear. Of course he wanted Zach to get well—more than anything. But he realized now that some corner of his mind *had* been building for the future, assuming he'd be able to keep seeing Zach even after the boy left the hospital. It was strange how quickly they'd bonded, but the bond was there just the same. Maybe it was because they had both lost fathers, although Zach's had been gone a long time. Or maybe it was the way Zach never talked about his illness, or how scared he had to be. Miguel wanted to protect him, to be a big brother to him . . .

"Believe it or not, I'm trying to help you," Howard said, a little more sympathetically. "Getting too attached will only make saying good-bye that much harder."

"I guess I just hadn't thought about that."

Howard smiled slightly. "Rookie mistake, and someday you'll know why. Okay, run and say hello to Zach, and then I'm going to introduce you to Petey Byer. I told him the two of you would watch cartoons."

"Are you kidding? You want me to sit around and watch TV?"

"He's five, Miguel, and he's scared. He just wants someone there so he's not alone. I can't be with him 24/7."

"I understand," said Miguel, still unable to believe he was going to be paid for watching cartoons. "Should I meet you out at the desk in, say, five minutes?"

Howard nodded as he left the lounge. "Be there or be square."

Miguel hesitated only long enough to put his chess set away. Then he strode off down the hall to see Zach.

"Miguel!" the pint-size patient greeted him. He was sitting up high in the bed, and as Miguel walked in he smoothed the blanket across his lap.

"I'm ready. You can put the chessboard right here." Zach paused. "Where is it?"

"I'm sorry," Miguel apologized guiltily. "I did bring it, but it's in the lounge. It turns out there are some other things I have to do today, and I'm not going to be able to play."

"But you promised!" Zach's eyes filled with tears. "What do you have to do?"

"A lot of things. You know there are other kids here, and they all need my time too. I'm really sorry to let you down, but I just shouldn't have promised."

Zach took a deep breath, sniffing back his disappointment. "I understand. You aren't really in charge."

"That's right," said Miguel, surprised by the boy's perception. On the other hand, Zach had spent more time at the hospital than he had. He probably knew things Miguel hadn't even figured out yet.

"Can we at least read some of our story?"

Miguel hesitated.

"Not even a whole chapter," Zach negotiated. "Just a few more pages."

Miguel looked toward the open doorway, then back at the boy on the bed. "Okay. I'll try. But not for a few hours. If I can, I'll come back before I leave and get you up to speed. All right?"

Zach smiled. "All right."

Miguel left the room uneasily, painfully aware that he had just made another promise he might not be able to keep. After the talk they'd just had, Howard was not going to be happy to find Miguel back in Zach's room the very same day.

Unless I do it after my shift, thought Miguel, seizing on a new idea. *If I'm off the clock, what can he say?*

That's what I'll do, he decided.

Howard had told him to spread himself out, and he would. During working hours, Miguel would make sure every patient got equal attention. But afterward, on his own time . . .

As long as I'm not neglecting the other kids, what harm can there really be in becoming attached to Zach?

"Excuse me, but if you insist on stepping off on the wrong foot, could you make sure it isn't mine?"

Wild laughter erupted around the black-haired beauty who'd spoken, and Nicole wished she could melt right through the gymnasium floor.

"I'm sorry," she murmured. "I didn't know you were going to go that way."

"Of course not. The whole *group* has only gone that way the last five times in a row. The whole group minus one, that is."

"I got confused."

You got confused, all right, she thought as she lined up again with the other eleven girls in her group. *You got confused the day you decided you had a chance of being a cheerleader.*

"All right, let's try it again," Melanie called from the front. "I'm going to slow it down, and this time try to stay with me. *One*, and *two*, and *three*, and *four* . . ."

For this, the second open practice, none of the groups were the same. Nicole had intentionally sought out an all-new set of girls—ones who hadn't seen her choke the first time. She might have thought twice, however, if she'd realized that Melanie was going to be her new leader. If there was anything worse than humiliating herself in front of strangers, it had to be humiliating herself in front of Melanie Andrews.

I would have to get Miss Perfect, thought Nicole, almost hating her again. *Why is everything in life so easy for some people?*

Melanie clicked through the steps of the dance they were learning like an extraordinarily graceful robot. Every movement, every turn was so sharp it was almost inhuman. Nicole did her best to imitate, but even though she turned in the right direction this time, she knew some of the other girls were doing better.

Oh, who am I kidding? All of them are doing better.

If only she could do the dance like Melanie! She'd be unbeatable then. Nicole tried to sharpen her movements, feeling like she was finally making some improvement at the slowed-down pace. But what would she do when they took things back up to tempo?

A whistle cut through the noise in the gym.

"It's five o'clock," Sandra's voice rang out. "That's all for today. We'll see you all back here next Tuesday."

Nicole refused to meet anyone's eyes as she changed her shoes on the lowest bench of the bleachers. She hadn't done quite so horribly this time, but she hadn't impressed anybody either—at

95

least not favorably. Her only consolation was that a few of the girls hadn't shown up, which she hoped meant they'd dropped out.

Goody. So now you can come in ninetieth instead of ninety-sixth.

The thing was, though, in her heart she still believed she could do it. If only she were learning under less stressful, less *crowded*, circumstances. If only things could move a little more slowly. She just didn't catch on the first second, like some girls, and then she got totally rattled.

I'll bet if Melanie would teach me privately I could really surprise a few people. She still might not make the squad, but at least she could walk away with her pride.

Nicole looked up from her shoelaces to spot Melanie laughing with Tanya on the other side of the gym. Thanks to all those fund-raisers with Eight Prime, Nicole did know her old rival a lot better now. Asking for a favor wouldn't be totally out of the question. . . .

Yeah, if I was asking to borrow a quarter or something . . . But I can't ask her this.

She would have to swallow a gallon of pride just to bring it up—and Melanie didn't like her enough to agree.

No, I'll just have to go it alone. Depressed, she threw her gym shoes into her bag, crept out a side door, and headed for home.

The moment Nicole got into the house, she ran up to her room to telephone Guy. Soon she'd be called down to dinner and the nightly exchange of insults with her younger sister, Heather, but before all that started she wanted someone to cheer her up.

Courtney's certainly not the one for the job, she thought as she dialed Guy's phone number. She had barely seen her friend since she'd broken the news about Jeff and Hope, and she certainly didn't want to talk about that again. *Besides, even if I can get her off the subject of Jeff for a minute, she'll just tell me cheerleading's stupid. That's Courtney's version of comfort.*

Not that Nicole planned to tell Guy about the cheerleading tryouts. For one thing, she had a sneaking suspicion that her making the squad wouldn't be at the top of his list of important things either. For another, if she didn't succeed, he never needed to know she had tried.

Guy picked up on the third ring. "Hello?"

"Hi. What are you doing?"

"Homework. You?"

"Nothing right now. We'll probably have dinner pretty soon." Nicole walked through her new dance steps as she talked, making a crooked path through the laundry strewn about her floor. "Tomorrow Eight Prime is having a sucker sale for St. Patrick's Day. Don't forget to wear green."

"Not likely. Our school uniform is green. Besides, I'm Irish."

"You are?"

"Well, as Irish as any American whose family has been here a few generations."

"I have some Irish blood too," said Nicole. "And English and German and I can't remember what all. I don't really care, to tell you the truth. I mean, we're all Americans now, so what difference does it make?"

"None. It's just fun to know."

There was a pause in the conversation while Nicole continued practicing her dance. With her cordless phone she could move across the room, but only one arm was free to do the hand motions. She snapped it through the positions, trying to imitate Melanie's crisp style. "I had fun the other weekend," she ventured.

She hadn't, but that was hardly Guy's fault. She was the genius who had begged him to double with Jeff.

"Me too. In fact, I was thinking maybe we could do something again this Saturday."

"Really? Okay." She wasn't about to tell him that was exactly what she'd been hoping for. "Except that this time, well . . . let's make it just us."

"You don't want to double?"

Not if I can avoid it. The last thing Nicole wanted was a repeat of the Hope experience. The girl actually seemed pretty nice, but if Nicole was obligated to hate her, she'd rather not hang out with her.

"I just think . . . uh . . . no. Not really."

Guy laughed. "Good. Me either."

Nicole had the first sixteen counts of the dance down perfectly now. She launched into them again, widening her steps until they were almost performance size. *One* and *two* and *three* and . . .

"So where are we going to go?" she asked. "I think it would be fun if wh—wh—whoooooaa!"

Her right foot had caught a sweater that her left one held pinned to the floor. Unable to untangle her feet in time, she lurched sideways under her own momentum, falling into her desk chair. The rolling chair careened away, crashing into the closet doors with a noise like a Nascar wreck. Nicole hit the floor in a heap.

"What was that?" Guy asked, alarmed. "Are you okay?"

"What? Oh. That wasn't me," Nicole lied quickly, scrambling back to her feet. "I mean it was, but it was just the chair. It was nothing."

"Are you sure?" Guy asked doubtfully.

"Of course. So what are we doing again?"

"Let me think of something. I'll pick you up at six, all right?"

"All right."

They talked a bit longer, and by the time Nicole

hung up she was reasonably certain that she'd smoothed over her little lapse in coordination. At least Guy hadn't mentioned it again. She tossed the phone onto her bed, pushed the chair back under the desk, and kicked some laundry out of her way, ready to practice in earnest.

"*One* and *two* and *three* and *four*," she counted, both arms into it now. "And *five* and *six* and . . . *Heather!* Get out of my room, you heinous little snoop! How long have you been standing there?"

Heather howled with laughter from behind the cracked-open bathroom door. "Long enough to see you make a total fool of yourself," she mocked, pushing it open the rest of the way. "*One* and *two* and *three* and *four*." Mincing around Nicole's room, she flapped her arms like a spastic windmill. "Oh, wait, I almost forgot the finale!"

Stumbling across the floor, Heather did an exaggerated, slow-motion fall into Nicole's desk chair, pushing it back into the closet. She dropped to the carpet, then immediately popped back up, taking several bows. "Thank you, thank you," she told her imaginary fans. "It's just a little something I whipped up. I call it 'Pom-poms for Brains.' "

"You creep!" shrieked Nicole. "I'm going to tell Mom you were spying on me!"

She charged for her sister, but Heather was quicker, scrambling out the door and onto the upstairs landing.

"Go ahead!" Heather taunted. "I could use a bigger audience." She tore down the stairs, waving her arms overhead like an ape. "And *one* and *two* and *three* and *four* . . ."

"*Mom!*" With a thunderous pounding of platform shoes, Nicole raced after her.

Eight

"Geez. Is it early enough for you?" Jesse complained to Ben. "I think we could have slept in a little longer."

Ben nodded, then quickly put a hand to his hair to make sure his new styling gel was holding. He had dressed extra carefully that day, and he didn't want to mess himself up in the first ten minutes. "It's better to be here first. That way we have a chance to sell to everybody."

Pushing open the side entrance door where he and Jesse were waiting, Ben strained to see around an outside corner of the main building. "Besides, I think I see some cars in the parking lot."

"Those are *ours*," Jesse grumbled.

There was no denying that Eight Prime had arrived at school early that morning, but no one was more eager to get rid of those disastrous green suckers than Ben. He'd have shown up in the dark, if he'd thought it would help.

Closing the door, he bent down beside his backpack, which he had left on the hall floor. Beside it was the cardboard box of suckers he and Jesse had been given at the Eight Prime meeting they'd attended just a few minutes before.

"There are four entrances to the main hall," Peter had told them. "I think we ought to split into pairs. Melanie and Nicole can take the front door, and Leah and Miguel the door to the quad. Jenna and I'll take one side, and that leaves the other for Jesse and Ben."

"I want the side by the parking lot," Ben had said immediately, sure it would see more action than the door closer to the bus stop and library.

"Fine."

Jenna had passed out the boxes of beribboned suckers, and the four sets of partners had gone their separate ways. Now Ben pawed through the box he and Jesse had been entrusted with, admiring the merchandise.

"We ought to put a couple of these on. You know, to give people the right idea. My treat." Fishing a dollar out of his pocket, Ben put it into the envelope taped inside the box.

"I'm not wearing anything with a bow," Jesse said, still slouching against the wall. "Forget about it."

"They don't all have bows." Ben held up two of the plain "guy" suckers, but Jesse wouldn't budge.

"Thanks, but no thanks. You wear them both."

"I can't wear them both—" Ben began, but just then the side door burst open, admitting its first group of students. Hurriedly pinning a sucker to his green cardigan, Ben grabbed a bulging handful and stood to greet his customers.

"St. Patrick's Day!" he shouted. "Luck of the Irish to you, but only if you wear green."

He held a couple of beribboned suckers out to some passing girls. "Only fifty cents each, or two for a dollar."

Two out of three of them stopped.

"How cute!" one exclaimed.

"Oh, no. Is it really St. Patrick's Day?" Her friend looked down at her pink shirt and blue overalls. "How could I forget?"

"Not a problem!" Ben assured her, holding one of the "girl" suckers against his own sweater for them to see. "Just pin this on, and you've got it covered."

"I'll take it," Overalls Girl said, digging through her backpack for change.

"Only a dollar for two," Ben reminded them.

"Give me two," said her friend, holding out a bill. "I'll give one to Cynthia."

"Oh, good idea. I'll get one for Gem."

Soon four or five people were waving dollars at him, and no one was asking for change. With the suckers only fifty cents apiece, everyone was taking two. Ben ran back to the box and exchanged the money he'd collected for two more handfuls of suckers. Jesse was already there, a big smile on his face.

"This is easier than kindergarten," he said, adding his money to Ben's. "Tell the guys to buy them for their mothers."

Ben stood up, eager to put the tip to use, only to find that the crowd had moved in to gather around the box.

"I want one of those cute suckers," a girl in front told him.

"Me too."

"Me too!"

"Back here!"

For the next ten minutes, Ben and Jesse sold side by side, almost as fast as they could take money. It seemed every girl who saw the suckers wanted one—or two—whether she was wearing green or not. They also sold a few of the "guy" suckers, but the ones with the bows were the definite winners. Ben dipped into the box again and again—until a vision in mint green cashmere walked in through the door.

"Angela!" he called, abandoning his post and running toward her. "Angela, happy St. Patrick's Day."

"You too, Ben," she said with a smile. "I see we both dressed for it."

"Yes, and this will go perfectly with your outfit."

Without asking permission, almost without thinking, he reached forward to pin a sucker on her coat.

"Wait! What are you doing?"

He froze in position. "Don't you like it?"

"I just want to know what it is."

Ben held it up for her to see, then cautiously reached forward again and began pinning it to her lapel. "We're selling these for the Junior Explorers, but you can have one for free."

"I'd rather pay for it. How much do they cost?"

"Don't worry. I already paid for that one." Which was true, because Jesse had never taken the one Ben had bought for him.

"Well . . . okay. Thank you."

Ben's hands were still bungling the pinning job. Angela's stopping him in the middle had really rattled him, and the added stress probably would have caused him problems even if he hadn't been seized by the sudden fantasy that it was prom night and he was pinning on her corsage. Would he ever have the courage to ask her to something like that? Or maybe the prom was too big. He ought to start smaller.

Shoving the pin back up through the fabric at last, Ben stood back to check his work. To his surprise, he hadn't done that badly. "There. What do you think?"

Angela glanced down. "Cute. Thanks, Ben. You're sweet." She flashed him a perfect cheerleader's smile before she walked off down the hall.

I'm sweet! Ben floated on air all the way back to the sucker box, where he found Jesse laughing at him.

"Somebody has a crush," Jesse teased. "Talk about lost causes!"

But Ben was far from discouraged as he resumed selling candy to the crowd.

Hadn't he just made Angela smile?

"You're lucky you found us!" Melanie called to a girl walking into the cafeteria. "Where's your green?"

"Oh, are you selling those cute suckers? I *am* glad I found you," the girl said, rushing over. She bought one and immediately pinned it to her white shirt. "There. Peace at last," she muttered as she walked off.

"This is even easier than this morning," said Nicole, who had just sold two of her own. "Everyone already knows about us."

Melanie nodded silently. She didn't hold any more animosity toward Nicole, but she couldn't help wishing she were working with Jesse instead. Not that he'd given her the least reason to hope for a reconciliation. That morning, he had taken off with Ben without a backward glance, as if he actually preferred Ben's company to hers. Ben!

"Hey, Melanie. How does that second sequence in the dance go again?" Nicole asked. "Do you kick with the right leg first, or the left?"

"The right."

Of course, hanging out with Nicole might have been more fun if the girl had wanted to talk about *anything* other than cheerleading tryouts. Not only was Melanie thoroughly sick of that subject, it wasn't fair to the other girls if Nicole got inside information.

"Would there be extra points for kicking high? Because I can kick really high."

"You'll lose points if you kick higher than the squad. You're supposed to be part of a team."

"Oh. Right. I meant I'd kick as high as the squad, only better."

Melanie forced a weak smile. Now Nicole wasn't even making sense.

"There sure are a lot of good dancers trying out."

"Mmm."

"I'm a pretty good dancer too, though. And, I mean, dancing isn't everything. You have to have the right look. Some of those girls . . . I can't believe what they show up to practice in. It's like they don't even care."

"Uh-huh."

"Do you think I . . . well, do I—"

"St. Patrick's Day suckers!" Melanie called to a passing clique, managing to unload the rest of the ones she was carrying.

"I'm going to go get some more from Jenna and

Leah," she told Nicole, escaping as fast as she could. It was one thing answering straightforward questions about the routines, but if Nicole was going to start fishing to find out how she compared to the other girls, Melanie didn't want to be near her. She headed for the nearest classroom building, where Jenna and Leah had staked out a quiet corner on the floor.

"Hey, there you are, Melanie," Leah called cheerfully as she approached.

The lunchtime teams had changed around slightly so that Leah and Jenna could tie bows onto all the remaining "guy" suckers. The suckers with ribbon were selling better, and if anybody needed one without, it was easy enough to slip the bow off.

"Did you sell all you had already?" Jenna asked.

"Nicole still has a few, and things are slowing down now that people are eating lunch, but I'll bet we get another rush when people start back to classes. Whoever has change left over . . ."

"We can barely keep up with you guys," Leah said happily. "Peter was already back here too, to get more for him and Miguel."

"Good." Melanie made a basket of the loose front of her shirt for Leah to fill. "Maybe we won't have to sell them after school then."

"Not at this rate," Leah agreed.

"All right. I'll see you guys later."

Melanie walked off with a shirt full of suckers, wishing she didn't have to head back to Nicole.

Well, if she asks me anything else about cheerleading, I'll just have to shut her down.

For one thing, she was supposed to be impartial. For another, she didn't want to hurt Nicole's feelings.

I mean, it's not like she's awful. But making the squad?

I don't think so.

"I can't believe it!" Peter whooped. "All gone!"

Classes had let out for the day only five minutes before, and he and Jenna had just sold the last green sucker.

"What a relief." Jenna removed the full money envelope from their box and handed it to him.

Peter put it in his backpack, along with the other three. There had been so few suckers left after lunch that it hadn't made sense to keep four teams on the job. Instead, he and Jenna had taken the final handful, along with the cash collected by everyone else.

"We sure owe Leah a thank-you for that corsage idea. If I'd had any idea how hot this would be, I'd have wanted to do it on purpose. I'd have paid more attention to Jesse's pricing suggestions, too."

Jenna shrugged. "The low price was what made things so easy."

"You're probably right. But still! I can't wait to pay Ben back for expenses and put the rest of this money in the Junior Explorers' savings account. We're finally in the black!"

"What a relief," Jenna repeated, slinging her backpack onto one shoulder.

Peter followed her out of the building, toward the student parking lot. "I feel like we ought to celebrate. Do you want to get ice cream? Or I'd love to drive you up to the lake. You haven't even seen the camp yet."

Excited by the idea, he turned to walk backward across the front grass, his eyes fixed on his girlfriend's face. "Let's go. You want to?"

"I can't. I'm on my way to the hospital."

"Do you have to go today?" he asked, disappointed. She'd been at the hospital every afternoon for weeks. Now that Sarah was out of danger, did Jenna really have to spend so much time there? After all, there were plenty of other Conrads in the clan.

"Sarah needs me."

Peter stopped walking. "*I* need you. It's not any fun planning things without you."

"Well, I'm sorry. There's such a thing as priorities."

Her words were a slap in the face. Did she think he didn't know that?

"Of course. And Sarah's the most important one. It's just . . ."

"What?"

That I feel like you're slipping away, he thought. *Like you don't care anymore. Is everything right between us? Because it sure doesn't feel that way.*

"Nothing," he said instead. "Tell Sarah I said hello."

Nine

This has gone on long enough, thought Nicole, hanging out by the end of the lunch line on Thursday. She'd barely seen Courtney lately, and she could no longer ignore the nagging suspicion that her best friend was mad at her.

At first it had been easy to make excuses. Nicole was busy; Courtney was licking her wounds after her recent humiliation. Nicole hadn't been inclined to push, for fear that Courtney would turn on her. Besides, it wasn't as if Courtney were hanging out with that awful Emily Dooley instead. Nicole had her eye on that situation, and every time she'd seen Emily the girl had been Courtney-free.

So Nicole wasn't *totally* worried . . . but she was worried enough to wait for her friend that day, hoping to eat with her. "Come on, Court. Where are you?"

Finally Courtney's unmistakable red head came into view among the crowd streaming into the cafeteria. Nicole started to hurry forward, then stopped, nonplussed. Courtney wasn't alone. Not only that, she was walking hand in hand with Kyle Snowden, the most notorious guy at school!

What is she doing? Nicole wondered, backing up quickly.

To say Kyle was handsome was an understatement. He was more like drop-dead gorgeous. Even so, his reputation for staying with a girl just long enough to seduce her was widely known. Nicole would have been afraid to stand next to the guy for fear of what people would say about her. Besides that, Kyle was tough. Really tough. Nicole and Courtney had seen him start a fight at a football game once. Nicole had even heard that he had a criminal record. That was only a rumor, but the fact that everyone was so ready to believe it ought to have been proof enough. Courtney herself had said that any girl who would go out with Kyle had better know self-defense. And unless she'd been taking secret karate lessons . . .

What is she thinking? Nicole didn't have a clue.

Falling back into the crowd, she watched as Courtney and Kyle joined the line. Courtney swaggered more than walked, her head held high and an enormous smile on her face. Nicole knew immediately that her friend was "making an entrance," aware of the eyes turning her way.

How did she even meet him? Nicole asked herself. *Maybe they aren't really together. But they're holding hands—they* must *be together.*

Not to mention the besotted look on Courtney's face. She was gazing at Kyle as if he'd replaced Jeff overnight.

She is on the rebound. Or maybe this is supposed to make Jeff jealous?

Nicole felt a wall bump into her from behind. She'd backed up as far as she could go. Rooted to the spot, she watched Courtney and Kyle with mounting dread.

They were whispering to each other in line, their heads close together. Courtney was giggling, and Kyle wore a suave smile as he trailed one teasing finger down her nose. Black hair and sky blue eyes, the guy even knew how to dress. In a situation like this, seeing him so clean and calm and Cupid-like, it was *almost* possible to forget having seen him smash someone's face. But how could Courtney forget the hearts he had smashed as well?

And then, while Nicole watched in horror, Courtney flung her arms around Kyle's neck and kissed him in full view of the cafeteria.

She's crazy!

Courtney had to know that everyone was watching, and in the unlikely event that anyone was missing it, they were sure to hear the gossip before that day's classes let out. A move like Courtney had just made was social suicide.

Or, more correctly, a move like Courtney was

making. Nicole felt her cheeks heat up as the kiss went on, becoming more and more passionate. Courtney and Jeff had never been much for kissing in public, and certainly Nicole had never witnessed a scene like *this*. Was this supposed to make Jeff jealous, or just embarrass everyone who saw it? Nicole wanted to look for Jeff, to see his reaction, but she was unable to tear her eyes away, watching with the same morbid fascination she'd have felt for a jumper on a high-rise ledge. Courtney might be out of her mind, but Nicole found the behavior before her unsettling in more ways than one.

She still hadn't kissed Guy yet. Not even a little peck, let alone the way Courtney was kissing Kyle. And as she watched her best friend lose herself to a total stranger, it occurred to Nicole that perhaps she ought to try it.

Nothing so uninhibited, of course. *Certainly* nothing so public. But just a kiss. A first kiss . . .

With an effort, she ripped her gaze away and focused on the ceiling.

Maybe I'll try it this weekend.

The moment the last bell rang on Friday, Ben ran for his locker, eager to find Mark. The two of them had a big weekend ahead, beta testing Mr. Pipkin's most recent video game, and Ben was truly excited to finally get a crack at it.

But it got better. His mother had let him drive her car to school that day for the first time ever. If he hurried, he could be seen in the student parking lot by the maximum number of people.

"Are you ready?" Mark asked. He was already at Ben's locker, a full backpack over his shoulders.

"I'm just going to drop off a few of these books." Ben spun out his combination like a pro, not wasting a movement. "There!" he said, slamming the locker door.

"I can't wait to see this thing," Mark told him as they followed the crowds out of the main building. "It's got astronauts, right? If it's even half as cool as Tomb of Terror—"

"Yeah, that was a good one," Ben said quickly, not wanting to talk about it. He had loved the Egyptian-theme adventure—but not all the trouble he'd gotten into because of it. "My dad swears this is even better."

"Cool! So which car is yours?"

Ben's eyes scanned the chaos in the parking lot. Students were swarming over the pavement, cars backing out in all directions. "That one," he said, pointing proudly. "Well, it's my mom's, anyway. Come on."

He unlocked both doors of the big sedan, hesitating as long as he could before actually getting in. *If only Angela would walk by and see me driving!*

But Ben didn't see any of the cheerleaders. *Maybe they have a practice*, he thought, trying not to feel let down. He had known all along that being seen by Angela was a major long shot.

"Do you want to go to The Danger Zone first?" Ben asked as he started the car. "My dad probably won't be home for a couple more hours, so we might as well warm up at the arcade."

Mark looked disappointed. "Oh. Well, all right. They don't have anything nearly as good as your dad's stuff, though."

No, but there will be a whole bunch of people there to see me drive up. And since he finally had a car to show off, he wanted to take full advantage.

Ben pulled out of the school parking space extra carefully, making sure to look first, signal, and check every mirror. Maybe he hadn't gotten the highest possible score on his driving test, but that was only because he had been so nervous during those last few stressful days. He knew he was a good driver, and he planned to prove it by never, ever having an accident, or even getting a ticket.

He made it to The Danger Zone with his record still squeaky clean, pulling into a space right in front. But inside the big, echoing arcade nearly all the games were deserted. No one was eating pizza on the picnic-bench-style tables in the center, either. Ben could look right through the empty building, out through the big front windows, and see his car sitting there by itself. He sighed. His triumphant entrance had gone completely unobserved.

"Good. No one's here. We can play whatever we want," said Mark, heading straight for his favorite Maniac Marauders station, in the corner.

"Yeah," Ben said sadly, tagging along. "I guess we're a little early."

Mark nodded as he fished for quarters in his front pocket. "Everyone will be here later. With dates."

"Yeah." Ben sighed again, wondering if he'd ever get to go to the school hangout with anyone besides Mark. Emptying the quarters out of his pockets, he added them to the ones Mark had stacked along the rail.

"We're going to need to break some dollars, but we might as well play these first."

"Yeah. Mark, if you wanted to ask a girl out, what would you say?"

Mark paused with a quarter halfway into the slot. "What girl?"

"Just a girl. Any girl."

"Well, I think it kind of matters who she is. I might do it one way for one girl, and another for somebody else."

"Really?"

Mark withdrew the quarter. "I might," he said defensively.

"I thought most guys had a plan for these things. You know, like some special trick. A gimmick."

"News to me," Mark said, making a face. "What is this all about, anyway? Are you asking someone out?"

"No," Ben said quickly. "I'm just speaking hypothetically."

"It's Angela, isn't it?" Mark hooted. "Oh, man. You are *crazy*! Girls like her don't date guys like us."

"I never said it was Angela!" Ben snapped, becoming flustered. With an effort, he lowered his voice. "I mean, I told you it wasn't anybody."

"Yeah, that's what you told me, all right." Mark was smiling slyly. He leaned back against the game, flipping a quarter between two fingers. "Let's see, if I was foolish enough to *hypothetically* want to date a *hypothetical* cheerleader, how would I ask her out?"

Ben was already sorry he'd ever mentioned it. "Let's just drop it and play the game."

"No, now you have me interested. What if you sent her flowers and had them delivered in one of her classes? You could ask her out on the card."

"I could." *If I wanted the entire school to know my business.* "Or maybe something a little less flashy."

"Less flashy? The girl is a cheerleader! Or, I mean," Mark corrected himself, laughing, "the *hypothetical* girl is *hypothetically* a cheerleader."

Boy, was Ben sorry he'd mentioned it.

"Oh! Oh, I know!" said Mark. "A singing telegram! You could have someone serenade her in the cafeteria."

That idea was even worse than the first one. If it failed, Ben would be a complete laughingstock. "I said *less* flashy."

"You're thinking too small. For a hypothetical girl like Angela, you need to go all out." Mark rubbed his chin with one finger. "Let's see. A blimp flashing her name? Skywriting? Oh! Take out an ad in the school paper! But not one of those cheesy little personals in the back. Get an entire page."

"Uh-huh." Ben managed to maneuver past his friend to drop some quarters into the game. The opening sequence began, mercifully distracting Mark from Ben's personal life.

"Prepare for defeat!" Mark said gleefully, stationing himself in front of a joystick.

Was that supposed to have some sort of double meaning? Ben wondered.

He took the other control, barely concentrating on the game. He should have known better than to ask Mark for advice about girls. The guy was as clueless as he was. Not one of his ideas had sounded doable to Ben. If anything, they had all seemed kind of lame.

And if they seem lame to me . . .

I should have asked Miguel. Or Jesse. Either one of them had tons more experience than Mark, so they were sure to have better advice. He'd been afraid that they'd make fun of him, though, and he hated looking foolish in front of Eight Prime.

121

So instead I got made fun of and got bad advice. Perfect.

"You know what you ought to do?" Mark said, still ripping away on his joystick. "Just ask her. Walk up and ask her. That's my best advice."

It *was* his best advice. And a moment later, Ben decided to take it.

After all, being timid never got me anywhere. It's time to take charge, like a man.

Or at least like a guy with a license.

"So what do you think?" Leah asked. "I know a condominium weight room probably doesn't spring to mind when most people think of a romantic evening, but nobody ever comes down here. I knew we'd have it all to ourselves."

"I like it," said Miguel, stretching out on the blanket Leah had spread in the dimmest corner. "The food was good, too."

"I'm glad."

After considering a lot of other, more conventional possibilities for her Friday-night date with Miguel, Leah had finally hatched the idea of a French-style picnic in the little gym on her building's ground floor. It had all the necessary elements: romance, privacy, and a reasonable price tag. And things had turned out well, if she did say so herself. Beneath the thick red blanket, yoga mats cushioned them from the floor. The lights in the room were off except for a couple of dim security lamps; their glow added nicely to the light from the candles Leah had brought. And spread out on the floor before them were the remains of a dinner that had included French bread, cheese, grapes, cold roast beef, and warm apple turnovers.

Leah put down a half-eaten pastry and stretched out beside Miguel. "A restaurant would have been prettier, but this is a lot more private."

"I don't know," Miguel said with a mischievous grin. "The view looks pretty good from here."

"You'd better say that." She rested her head against his chest. It rose and fell with his breath, a little ship at dock. The moment was perfect. Everything was right. Turning her face up toward his, she closed her eyes and waited for him to kiss her.

"You know what Zach said today?"

Leah opened her eyes. "What?"

"That he liked me the best of anyone in the hospital."

"I'm not surprised. Reading him books, teaching him chess . . . he's lucky to have you." Closing her eyes again, she wriggled a little closer.

"I hope he's going to be all right."

Leah held her position. "Me too," she murmured. She felt Miguel shift his weight, moving his head toward hers.

Then he shifted it back. "And you thought Zach was too young to learn chess! He's a whiz at it."

With a sigh, she opened her eyes. "My mistake."

"Working at the hospital is just so cool! I mean, I liked working for Mr. Ambrosi, but this is so much better."

"Yes, it is."

So maybe she'd had something else in mind for the rest of the evening, something a little more romantic. But if Miguel wanted to talk about his new job instead, she supposed she should be glad. She was still so relieved that he *had* a new job that she couldn't be offended. "You still want to be a doctor?"

"More than ever. I wish you could meet Dr. Wells. He's so cool. I went on rounds with him again today—oh, and Lucy got discharged! Her mother brought a cake and we had a little party in the playroom for all the kids who could get there. Howard made a puppet out of a rubber glove. I know it sounds stupid, but he did this really funny show with it. All the kids were laughing their heads off. And then, after that . . ."

Leah snuggled in his arms as the stories went on and on, perfectly content. His voice hummed in her ears, deep and soothing. How could she be anything other than happy, when he'd found a career he cared so much about? And, of course, there was a certain irony to the situation that she couldn't overlook.

I always knew Miguel could be talkative if he wanted to.

Ten

"I don't even know why we let the kids paint," Peter said grouchily, wringing his shirt out over the sink in the park activities center. "This happens every time."

Chris chuckled as he reached under Peter's arms to drop some brushes into the water. "Yeah. It happens every time *you* mix paint. The kids don't have anything to do with it."

"Why does someone always have to have brown?" Peter complained. "No matter what they paint, there's always something that absolutely, positively, has to be brown. It's not like you can tell what half these pictures are anyway. What's wrong with red? Or blue?"

He gave his shirt one last, vicious wrench, forcing out more drops of water, then stuffed it into a plastic grocery bag he'd found. Now he was shirtless, but the last of the kids had already left with their parents, and he could wear his jacket over bare skin long enough to get home.

"Maybe we could convince the kids to paint with plain water, like in those magic coloring books."

"That's not going to work," Peter began irritably. "Those books have special . . . oh." Chris's face made it clear he'd been kidding. "I'm sorry. I'm not in a very good mood today."

"Really? I hadn't noticed," Chris said dryly. Leaning back against the counter, he gave Peter his full attention. "What's up?"

"Nothing." Peter sighed. "Everything. I don't know. I just have a lot on my mind right now."

"Like what?"

"Like camp, and who's going to drive the—" Peter cut himself off, not wanting Chris to think he was accusing him.

"The bus. Yeah, I've been thinking about that too. I'll be able to drive it sometimes, but . . . isn't Miguel almost eighteen? Or what about Leah? Maybe one of them can get the right license before summer."

Peter thought a minute before he answered. "I can ask."

He didn't have a lot of hope, though. Miguel was always busy, and Peter couldn't see Leah being available to drive the bus all summer either.

If only I were old enough! But since he was only sixteen, even his summer birthday wouldn't help him.

"I guess what's really bothering me is Jenna," Peter admitted, running more water over the brushes. "I thought once Sarah was out of danger, Jenna would

126

pitch in and help me with Junior Explorers again, but she barely seems interested."

Chris looked surprised. "Did she say that?"

"Not in so many words. She's just acting . . . I don't know. Really weird."

For a moment, the only sound was the splashing in the sink.

"I think you have to cut her some slack," Chris said at last. "At least until Sarah gets out of the hospital. Is that going to be pretty soon?"

"It can't be soon enough. I know I sound totally selfish, but that just makes things worse. I miss my girlfriend. And because of the circumstances, I'm not even allowed to say so."

Chris nodded. "I think I understand now. But you know Jenna is probably pretty worn out with all the worrying she's been doing. Have you tried just hanging out with her? Not talking about Sarah, not talking about camp, just hanging out?"

Peter opened his mouth to say that he *had* tried, and that Jenna was always too busy. But a moment later he realized he hadn't. Ever since the accident, every time he'd seen Jenna the conversation had been about one of those two things, if not both.

"What about a matinee?" Chris suggested. "Or even an afternoon of television? Something totally mindless, where no one has to talk if they don't want to."

"You know, that's not a bad idea," Peter said slowly.

He could already see it, in fact: He and Jenna relaxing on the sofa in his darkened den, a rented movie in the VCR. He could make popcorn, and get some Red Vines and those ice cream bonbons, just like in the theater. And he and Jenna *wouldn't* have to talk—holding hands would be enough. Just to be near her again, to sit by her side. Just the two of them...

For the first time that day, Peter felt a real smile coming on. "You know what, Chris? You just might be a genius."

"We've got the lane for another fifteen minutes," Guy said, motioning Nicole back to her feet. "Come on. If we hurry, we can bowl one more game."

"I'm really tired," she said, sliding lower on the bench. "And these shoes are giving me a blister."

Not to mention a headache from the way they clash with my outfit. What kind of twisted sadist designs bowling shoes, anyway?

"You're tired?" Guy laughed with disbelief. "We haven't even been here two hours."

Which is almost two hours longer than I wanted. Even if she'd liked bowling—which she didn't—it wasn't exactly her idea of a hot date. *Is it anybody's idea of a hot date?*

For that matter, were she and Guy even dating? They went out together, but for all the romantic interest he'd shown, she might as well be his little sister. If he *was* interested, she appreciated that he wasn't rushing her, but at this rate she'd have gray hair before they ever kissed.

"Well?" he prompted.

"I think I hurt my thumb," Nicole said pathetically. "You play. I'll watch."

Guy looked longingly toward the upright pins at the end of the lane, then back at Nicole. "That's all right," he said, sitting down beside her. "Let me see your thumb."

There was absolutely nothing wrong with her thumb, but what else could she do? She held it out, trying to look as if she actually expected him to find something.

Guy rolled it gently back and forth between the fingers of one hand. "It's a little red, but it doesn't look swollen. Let me see the other one."

He reached for her left hand, holding her thumbs side by side. At first she watched as he compared them, knowing he wouldn't find anything. But then her eyes traveled up his arms to his face, and her heart started beating faster.

They were finally holding hands—sort of—and his skin felt warm on hers. Guy's blue eyes were lowered to his task, his russet hair falling over them. Nicole suddenly wondered what her own hair looked like. Was it messed up? Was her makeup melted and running down her face? If it was, would Guy even notice?

Glancing over her shoulder, she noticed that the people in the lane next to them had left. She and Guy had the first lane, on the end of the building farthest from the snack bar, so for the moment there was no one right around them. Then, all of a sudden, the main alley lights went dim and colored strobes flashed back and forth across the lanes.

"It's Saturday night!" a hidden announcer declared. "Time to party!"

Music blared from overhead speakers while people continued their games, bowling toward the lit-up pins.

"Great," said Guy, pulling her hands closer to his face. "Now I can barely see."

Nicole's pulse pounded as fast as the music. She could feel his breath on her skin. Her fingers curled around his hands. They were so close. . . .

This was it—he *had* to kiss her now. She leaned forward, oblivious to everything else around them.

Then Guy let go of her thumbs and her hands fell straight to the bench. "Sorry, but I can't see anything wrong. I think you're probably okay, don't you?"

"What? Oh. Yeah."

Guy gave her a questioning look. "You don't sound too happy about it."

He isn't going to kiss me. The shock of disappointment nearly made her numb. How could he pass up a perfect chance like this? And if not now, then when? Ever?

130

He's never going to make a move. Unless I make one first.

Leaning closer, barely breathing, Nicole brought her face to his. She focused on his mouth as their lips inched closer together. Guy sat as if frozen, moving neither forward nor back. At the very last second, Nicole closed her eyes.

No guts, no glory.

Her lips pressed his, right on target. They yielded to hers, soft and warm, and for a moment Nicole felt a rush of triumph. She had done it!

Then Guy pulled away abruptly. Her eyes flew open in panic.

"What's the matter?" she asked breathlessly.

"I'm just . . . kind of surprised."

"Surprised in a good way, I hope."

"Well . . . I don't know."

"You don't *know?*" Nicole could feel the color rising in her cheeks. "What do you mean, you don't know?"

"It's not that I don't like you, Nicole. I like you a lot." He shrugged. "I just don't think I'm ready to take things to that level yet."

Not ready? she thought, completely at a loss. *Isn't it the girl who's supposed to be ready? What kind of lame excuse is that?*

"Don't be embarrassed," he said, patting her on the knee.

She wasn't embarrassed—she was mortified.

131

Nothing like this had ever happened to her before. It wasn't as if she went around kissing a lot of guys, for one thing. And it had never even occurred to her that she needed to wait for one to be "ready."

A vision of Courtney and Kyle in the cafeteria passed through Nicole's muddled brain. She had spoken to Courtney on the phone since then, and she was certain that readiness had never been an issue where Kyle Snowden was concerned.

"Why should I be embarrassed?" Nicole retorted. The last thing she wanted Guy to know was that her feelings were hurt too. He could say he liked her all he wanted, but if his actions didn't show it . . .

"You shouldn't. Let's forget about it." Rising from the bench, Guy began looking around for his shoes.

I'll forget about it. Maybe I'll forget all about it, Nicole thought sullenly, watching him with lowered eyes.

Whatever Guy's problem was, she didn't have to be part of it. And if he didn't want to kiss her, then maybe it was time to find someone who did.

Not a sleaze like Kyle, of course. But just a nice guy. A regular guy.

There has to be something in the middle.

All right. Get in, get the combo, and get out, Melanie thought, trying to psych herself up. Her father was in the poolhouse, presumably out of commission for the night, but she definitely didn't want to be caught

132

going through his desk. With one last breath for courage, she ducked through the study door.

Compared to other rooms in the Andrewses' house, the study was on the small side. Square and lined in dark wood, its main feature was a massive antique desk facing the door. A dark leather chair sat behind the desk, with a credenza behind that. Several of Mrs. Andrews's paintings hung on the walls to lighten the mood, a necessity in this room without windows. The visual reminder of her mother reassured her slightly as Melanie began her search.

Her father kept a compulsively neat office. The habit had long seemed strange to her, considering the disarray the rest of his life was in, but it could only make things easier now. Pulling open the first file drawer in the desk, Melanie began tabbing through labeled folders: Auto Insurance, Auto Maintenance, Auto Purchases, Auto Sales, Business Contacts . . .

They're alphabetical, she realized. *That's going to make things easier.* She pulled open the other file drawer in the desk, then turned to the drawers in the credenza, finding the S's in the last one. No "Safe."

All right. I guess that would have been too easy. If I could find the combination that way, so could a burglar.

Her father had obviously thought ahead. So what would the combination be under? Fire Insurance? Household Equipment? Miscellaneous? Hurriedly Melanie flipped through those files, as well as a few others. None of them had names that clearly included the safe, and all of them were stuffed. Her anxiety grew as she paged through the reams of mismatched papers with no luck, not even sure exactly what she was looking for. Would there be a brochure, a sheet of paper, a scrap? What if the combination wasn't even in the files?

Abandoning the file drawers, Melanie turned her attention to the shallow ones: pens, pencils, paper clips, stamps, envelopes, scissors, rubber bands, paper, a business card directory . . . She went through them all with impatience and a growing feeling that she was intruding on her father's privacy. She didn't want to be a snoop—she just wanted one little thing.

Why can't I find it?

Desperate, she pulled the pencil drawer completely out of the desk and examined the wood on the underside. Would her dad have written the combination somewhere hidden like that?

She checked a couple more drawers and even crawled under the desk before she gave up on that idea. A single slip of paper somewhere in the midst of so many would be a better hiding place. After another fifteen minutes of rummaging, however, she had to admit defeat. Wherever the combination was, it wasn't anyplace obvious, and she had neither the time nor the nerve to go through every paper in every file. Putting things back where she had found them as well as she could, she switched off the study light and made her escape, slipping silently up the staircase to her bedroom.

Now what?

She looked around her, at a loss. She'd probably never have a better chance to search, but she'd still come up with nothing. What was she supposed to do next?

I don't know. I can't even think about it any more right now.

She wandered to her picture windows, but it was dark outside and all she saw was her own reflection. She pulled the blinds savagely, not wanting to look. She was sick of herself, and of everything that went with being her.

Here it is, Saturday night, and I'm hanging around the stupid house, by myself, wondering about things I already ought to know. Why didn't Mom just tell me about Trent? Unless there was nothing to tell. Unless I'm just chasing shadows.

She dropped onto her bed, tired and depressed. *It wouldn't be the first time.* Glancing at the clock, she wondered what everyone else she knew was doing.

They're probably all on dates, she thought, made even more disgusted by her own pathetic state.

Not that she couldn't get a date if she wanted to. She could get a date just walking through the quad. There was a certain way of looking at a guy that was almost guaranteed to result in an immediate invitation—and there was another way of looking that made any romantic thoughts he might have had wither up and die. She'd been using that second look a lot lately. Maybe more than she should have. She couldn't wait for Jesse forever.

I'm not waiting for Jesse, she thought irritably. *I'm waiting to get over him.*

Although, she had to admit, there didn't seem to be much of a difference.

Her eyes drifted to the cordless phone on her nightstand. Was Jesse out with someone that night? She hadn't seen him with anyone lately, but that didn't mean a thing. Jesse could get a date just walking through the quad too.

On impulse, Melanie decided to give him a call. Picking up the phone, she punched the speed-dial button for his number quickly, before she could change her mind. Maybe she was crazy, but she was already feeling so low, it was hard to imagine what additional damage Jesse could do. Assuming he was even home.

To her amazement, he picked up on the second ring.

"Hi, it's Melanie," she said quickly. "What are you doing?"

"Not much. Hanging out. You?" His voice was casual, but she could tell he was surprised to hear from her.

"The same. I just finished up some stuff." Weak, but better than letting him think she was completely without a plan.

"Yeah, um, me too."

"So . . . I guess the sucker sale went well. Ben seemed pretty relieved."

Jesse snorted. "Only Ben could screw up something as simple as buying red suckers. I'd be relieved too, if I were him. Thank God I'm not!"

"I don't know. He has his license now, so he's doing better than me."

"In one of ten million areas."

Melanie smiled and changed the subject. "Are you going to California for spring break?"

"When is that? Next week already?"

"Like we're all not counting the days."

"I might have been, if I were going to Malibu. But that fell through. Again. Of course." He sighed discontentedly.

"What happened?"

"My brothers both made other plans, so now my mom wants me to wait until summer, when I can stay longer. You know, the same old thing," he said, sounding cynical.

"Oh. But I'll bet Brittany's glad you're staying."

"I guess so. It's . . . kind of complicated."

Melanie sensed a story he didn't want to tell her. "You guys are still getting along, though?"

"Sure."

"She was so cute at the Eight Prime meeting the other night, hanging out with her big bro."

"Mmm."

An awkward, nothing-to-say silence descended. Melanie wondered if he could possibly be thinking the same thing she was—that they were both alone that night, both lonely. It would be such an easy thing to get together . . . if she weren't the only one who wanted it.

"Well, I guess I don't have much to say," she admitted at last. "I just called to say hi. I didn't even know if you'd be home."

"You don't need a reason to call me," he said, in a way that made her heart beat faster. "I mean, I know there's been some bad stuff between us, but . . . we're friends now, aren't we?"

"Yes," she agreed, her pulse returning to its previous, sluggish rate. "Friends."

"I'm glad you called."

"You are?" She perked up a little again.

"Sure. Call anytime."

"All right."

She hung up the phone not knowing what to think. Jesse had said they were friends. But had he been hinting at something more?

Did she even still want something more?

"Ughhh, it's too complicated," she moaned,

holding her head and falling backward onto the pillows.

But at least he wasn't mad at her anymore, and if "friends" was what he was offering, she'd take it and try to be glad.

For such a popular girl, she sure didn't have very many.

Eleven

"Hello," Leah said cheerfully, sticking her head into Sarah's room late Sunday morning.

"Hi!" Jenna and Sarah said simultaneously. Caitlin smiled shyly.

Mrs. Conrad waved from beside Sarah's bed. "Hello, Leah. Come on in."

"Miguel and I are just dropping by," Leah explained as she joined them. "He's visiting another friend of his on the floor."

"Zach," Sarah said knowingly. "Miguel comes by sometimes, and he told me about him."

She was looking tons better than the last time Leah had seen her. Sitting up in bed with a wedge of pillows behind her, she had regained her color and had shed most of the tubes and monitor wires. Her blond hair was clean and shiny. The only thing obviously wrong with her now was the lump the external frame on her broken leg made under her hospital blanket.

"That's right," Leah said. "Those two have really hit it off."

"It would do you good to get out of here for a while

and stretch your legs," Mrs. Conrad told Jenna. "Why don't you girls go get some hot chocolate or something? Take a walk around."

Jenna stood up and took some money her mom handed her.

"Bring me back a pudding," Sarah directed before they walked out.

"She looks fantastic," Leah said as the elevator descended. "Is she almost out of here?"

Jenna nodded. "Almost. She'd probably be home already, except for the problems she's having walking."

"Do they know if she's going to keep limping?"

The doors opened on the first floor. A sign pointed the girls toward the cafeteria.

"She's got a physical therapist working with her now, but . . ." Jenna shook her head. "They don't know."

"I'm sorry."

Jenna took a deep breath, but when she smiled her expression was sincere, the old Jenna. "Thanks. But we're a long way from beaten. She'll keep having therapy, and she'll keep getting better. Maybe someday we won't even be able to tell. And if we can . . . so what? She's alive."

"Kind of puts things into perspective, huh?"

"Exactly."

They walked through the food line in the cafeteria. Leah chose hot tea while Jenna picked up a hot chocolate for herself and tapioca pudding for Sarah.

At a table in the corner, Jenna slurped her melting whipped cream while Leah dipped her tea bag up and down, trying to think of a way to broach the subject most on her mind.

"So," she opened at last. "I guess there's not so much reason for you to be here all the time now, is there? I mean, Sarah's almost well. And there's all the rest of your family . . . If you wanted to, you could more or less go back to a normal life."

All the animation went out of Jenna's face. "I like being here."

"Sure. But have you . . . have you talked to Peter yet about . . . you know."

Jenna shook her head rapidly, her eyes on her hot chocolate. "I can't."

Leah had suspected as much. Jenna wasn't at the hospital because she needed to be—not anymore. She was there to avoid her own life.

"You have to, Jenna. What are you going to do? Just not talk to him forever?"

"Not about that."

"Oh. That sounds like a good plan." Leah raised her eyebrows, trying to make her friend see the light.

"I know," Jenna said with a sigh. "I ought to tell him I'm still upset that he kissed Melanie. But I wouldn't even know how to bring it up at this point. It's too hard."

"I probably wouldn't want to bring it up again either," Leah said slowly. "But there is one obvious alternative."

"There is?" Jenna's eyes were eager as she leaned forward. "What?"

"You *could* just forget the whole thing."

Jenna sat back, disappointed. "Don't you think I've been trying? But I can't. It's impossible."

"Well, you have to do something. Do you think you could talk to Melanie?"

"About this? No way!"

"I just thought, well . . . if Melanie told you there was nothing between them . . ."

"Peter already told me that."

"But you don't believe him."

"So you think I'll believe *her*? Would you?"

"I don't know," Leah admitted.

"It's not even that I'm mad at him so much anymore as . . . well . . ." Jenna's voice was choking up. "He kissed Melanie *Andrews*, Leah. That's most guys' fantasy, isn't it? As good as it ever gets? How am I supposed to compete with that?"

"I don't think you need to compete—"

"It just makes me feel really weird," Jenna said, stabbing her whipped cream with a coffee stirrer. "I can't explain."

She didn't need to. Leah had experienced enough insecurity over Sabrina to recognize the same problem in one of her friends.

"I think I know how you feel. I do. But I also know that things can't go on like this. You have to do something, Jenna."

Ever since she'd found out about their kiss, Leah had felt awkward around both Peter and Melanie, never knowing what to say, or even where to look. Worse, she couldn't help worrying how it all would end.

Because if Jenna and Peter broke up, what would hold Eight Prime together?

"You're right," said Jenna. "*Something* has to change."

"I'm sure you and Peter can work this out. I mean, it's not like you two are going to break up, or anything crazy like that."

Leah tried to keep her voice light, as if the mere possibility were laughable, but the look in Jenna's eyes felt like ice water down her spine.

Jenna shrugged, then turned away. "I just don't know," she answered.

"Kung pao chicken!" Zach cried excitedly. "Miguel, where did you get this? They'll never let me eat it. What if I hurl?"

"It's all right," Miguel said with a chuckle. "I already cleared it with the nurses."

Miguel had driven to Leah's after mass, and the two of them had stopped at Paper Dragon on their way to the hospital. Now Miguel pushed the bed tray over Zach's lap and helped him open two waxed paper cartons—one for the chicken and one for fried rice.

"*Bon appétit*," he said, handing Zach a plastic fork. "I don't know how they say that in Chinese."

"Kung pao," Zach guessed, his mouth full of spicy chicken.

"Works for me."

Miguel pulled up a chair, smiling as he watched Zach eat. Because of the chemotherapy and resulting nausea, Zach was served mostly soft, bland food. The idea was to keep the vomiting to a minimum, but there was no harm in spicier fare—if Zach could keep it down.

"This is the best!" Zach raved. "Thanks, Miguel."

"You're welcome. Pretty soon you'll be getting out of here, and then you'll be able to eat Chinese as much as you like."

He didn't mention the surgery that would have to take place first. He was doing his best not to think about that.

Zach gave him that skeptical look again. "They're never going to let me back on the soccer team, though."

"What? Why not?"

"Because I'll be lousy. I started having trouble even before I had to come in here. And now that I've been here so long I'll be even worse. Soccer's a hard sport, you know—there's lots of running around."

"They have to let you back on the team," said Miguel, silently vowing to make them, if need be. "Everyone is going to be so glad to have you well that no one will expect you to be a star the first day."

"Star!" Zach rolled his eyes. "I'll be lucky if I can kick the ball."

"You'll just need to practice, that's all. I'll practice with you, if you want."

"Do you play soccer?" Zach asked excitedly.

"Uh, not really," Miguel admitted. "But you can teach me, can't you?"

Zach laughed. "I really like you, Miguel."

"Yeah?" The words made him feel ten feet tall. "I really like you, too."

He hung out awhile longer, tossing out the licked-clean cartons and playing a game of chess with Zach. When he finally rose to go, Zach didn't want him to leave.

"Can't you stay until my mom comes?" Zach begged. "She'll be here pretty soon."

Miguel checked his watch, seeing the time with a jolt. He had already overstayed the hour he and Leah had agreed to.

"Sorry. I have to meet my girlfriend. But I'll be back tomorrow. We'll do something then."

Zach made a face. "You have a *girlfriend*?"

"Yes. Are you very disillusioned?"

"I guess not. You're pretty old," Zach said, shrugging off the distasteful news. Miguel nearly laughed at the obvious effort it cost him.

"Okay. I'll see you tomorrow, then."

Walking hurriedly down the hall, Miguel checked the waiting room for Leah but didn't find her. He was on his way to check Sarah's room when Dr. Wells came around a corner.

"Miguel! I didn't see you on the schedule today."

"I'm not. I just stopped by to, uh . . ." He hesitated, hoping Dr. Wells wouldn't deliver a Howard-style lecture. "To, uh, see Zach. The nurses said it was okay if I brought him some Chinese food."

"Sure. Fine. I didn't even know he liked Chinese."

"He likes it spicy, actually."

Dr. Wells laughed. "He may not like it as much if it comes back up, but that's how we learn. Listen, I've been meaning to ask you, what college will you be attending? Do you have all your replies back yet?"

Miguel felt his insides shrivel. "Well . . . not exactly. I haven't applied anywhere yet."

Dr. Wells's face looked shocked. "What are you waiting for? It's very late, Miguel."

"I know." *Believe me, I know*, he felt like adding. Hadn't Leah delivered the exact same lecture a hundred times? "It's just that things are complicated, with my mom's health and all. Or at least they were until recently."

He hesitated, embarrassed to bring up money, but he wanted the doctor to know that he wasn't just a flake. "Finances are kind of tight for us too. I do intend to go to college, but how I'll pay for school is still kind of a mystery."

"The first thing you have to do is apply, Miguel." Dr. Wells laid a hand on his shoulder and stared intently into his eyes. "And at this stage it's better to be enrolled anywhere than nowhere. Besides, it doesn't much matter where you do your general ed."

"Right," Miguel said, a little dubiously.

Dr. Wells squeezed his shoulder. "The money is always there for motivated students who work hard and need it. Don't let finances make your decision for you."

"Well . . . I do have an application for CU lying around the house."

"There you go! Clearwater University is a great place to start. But you have to start, Miguel. You have to turn in the application."

"Right. I'll do that. I'll, uh . . . do it soon."

Dr. Wells dropped his hand and nodded. "Okay. And if you need any help, or advice on picking a major, call me anytime."

Miguel watched as the doctor bustled off. "Thanks," he called belatedly.

The doctor waved over one shoulder and continued on his way.

"Well, I guess that's settled, then," Miguel said under his breath.

He shook his head, still reeling. "I guess I'm going to CU."

Peter glanced around the Altmanns' den, satisfied. The movies he had rented were on the coffee table, next to the Red Vines and a dish of M&M's. The microwave popcorn, ice cream bonbons, and ice-cold sodas were ready and waiting in the kitchen. Now all he needed was Jenna.

He had seen her at church that morning. She had said she was going to the hospital after the service, but she had to be home by now.

"Mom! I'm going," he called on his way to the front door. "Back in a few minutes."

"All right," her answer floated back.

Driving to the Conrads' house, Peter rehearsed what he wanted to say. *I have to phrase this just right, or she's probably going to say no.* He could imagine her excuses: homework, chores, prior commitments with her sisters. *I have to make it clear that I'm not taking no for an answer. Everything's all set up, and she needs this. We* need *this.*

By the time he knocked on her door, however, Peter was ridiculously nervous. Why should a simple visit to his best friend have him so on edge? he wondered.

Because it wasn't simple. Nothing seemed simple anymore.

Maggie opened the door. "Jenna! It's Peter," she bellowed, waving him inside before running off into the house.

Peter stepped into the entry, reassured. Nothing had changed between him and Maggie, at least. He waited there alone until Jenna appeared on the stairs.

"Hi!" he said cheerfully. "Everything good with Sarah today?"

She shrugged as she hit the last step. "Pretty good, I guess."

"Get your coat and tell your parents you're coming to my house for a few hours. I've got something special planned."

Jenna's eyebrows went up, and not in a positive way. "What is it?"

"You'll see. You just have to come."

"I don't think I can," she said, shaking her head. "I just got home and I need—"

"To relax," Peter put in quickly. "You can't keep on the way you've been going. Come on over, Jenna. I promise it'll be fun."

She crossed her arms over an old thermal shirt, the kind with the little bow at the neck. Her jeans were loose and faded, her feet stuffed into slippers. She didn't look ready to go anywhere. More importantly, she didn't look like she wanted to.

"Jenna, please. We never do anything together anymore."

"Well, I'm sorry about that," she said sarcastically. "But I've been a little busy."

"I know you have. And that's why I wanted to do something nice for you. Something for both of us, actually."

She glanced toward the back of the house, in the direction of the kitchen. "My mom's going to be home soon, and I'm going to help her make dinner."

Peter was pretty sure he had already lost the fight, but he wasn't going down easily. "Can't Caitlin help instead?

"You should have asked me before you planned anything."

"I wanted to surprise you."

"Well, that's the problem with surprises. Sometimes they don't work out."

"Just tell me what you're doing right now. Right this minute."

"I just barely got home, Peter. I haven't had time to do anything besides change my clothes."

"What were you *about* to do, then?"

She hesitated just long enough to convince him she didn't have anything important on her schedule.

"You want to know what I had planned? I rented some movies and got all kinds of snacks, and I thought we could hang out together in my den, just the two of us. I promise I won't mention camp, or any kind of fund-raising. It'll be just like old times."

She smiled slightly. For a moment, he thought she was going to say yes.

"You should have asked me," she repeated. "I'm not in the mood right now."

"You're *never* in the mood," he said, more loudly than he had intended. Jenna's eyes darted toward the living room, and Peter hoped her father wasn't in there. He lowered his voice, attempting to sound calm. "It's just that lately you act like I barely even exist, Jenna. Even when we're together."

She wouldn't meet his eyes.

"What's up with that?"

"I think you're imagining things."

"Then prove it. Get your coat."

"I already told you, I have to cook dinner." There was a brittleness to her voice that said he was pushing too hard.

But Peter was so worked up that he couldn't let it go. "Yes, you did. What you didn't tell me is that you *want* to come. That you wish you could. Or even that you'd like to get out of cooking. I'm not hearing any of that, and I'm not seeing it, either."

Jenna's eyes flashed angrily. "Maybe I *don't* want to get out of cooking. It's Sunday afternoon, and my family's been practically torn apart for the last month. Maybe I *would* rather be here with them, enjoying a seminormal day. You're not the only thing in my life, you know."

Her voice had gone up a level. They were on the verge of a major fight.

Peter thought of all the things he could say: *I know. You make that perfectly clear.* Or, *What are you talking about? I'm not even in your life.* But some sixth sense warned him that any comeback he made now could be his last. Instead he took a deep breath and tried to be mature.

"Jenna, are you mad at me about something? Because I feel like you are, but I don't know what I've done."

"Why would I be mad at you?"

Peter could only think of one reason—and hadn't they already ruled that out? "I asked you first."

"I'm not mad at you, Peter. I mean, I'm a little bit upset right this minute, but that's because I'm tired and I look terrible and you just show up on my doorstep and expect me to do whatever you want. I have a mind of my own, you know."

"So before I came over here today you weren't mad at me in the slightest?"

"Did I say I was?"

"The problem isn't what you've been saying, Jenna."

"I'm not mad at you, all right? I just want to stay home."

Peter didn't know whether to believe her or not. But unless he was prepared to call her a liar, what else could he do?

"All right. I guess I'll see you at school tomorrow." He turned to leave, his hand tight on the doorknob.

"Peter, wait." Her voice behind him was small, contrite. "I'm sorry about the movies. I wish . . . well . . . Maybe another time."

He turned back to face her, wanting more than anything to wrap her into a hug and squeeze her hard. She seemed half willing. But something in her eyes held him back.

"Another time. Sure."

The door smacked shut behind him, the most final sound in the world.

Twelve

Okay, Ben thought nervously, wiping his palms down the front of his jeans. *Plan your work, and work your plan.*

The saying didn't apply exactly, but it was the best one he could come up with as he lurked by Angela's locker, waiting for her to appear before lunch. He had made up his mind to ask her out that day—no matter what—and he wanted to do it there instead of in the cafeteria, in front of the other cheerleaders.

Not even an option, he thought, quailing at the mere idea.

Not that asking her in the hall was going to be a lot better. Even if she came to her locker alone, there were still people everywhere, just waiting to mock him if he failed. If only there was some way to get her to go out with him without actually having to ask her! He was tempted to skulk off and think more about that angle when Angela suddenly showed up.

"Hey, Ben. What are you doing here?" Motioning for him to stand to one side, she began dialing her combination.

"I, uh, well . . . I was waiting for you," he admitted.

"You were? How come?" She didn't seem to suspect a thing as she slung her backpack off her shoulder and started transferring books between it and her locker.

Ben glanced right and left, to assess how many people were listening. A couple of jocks joshed each other behind him—a shy-looking girl rummaged through her locker on Angela's other side. He would have liked a little more privacy, but if he waited any longer Angela was likely to leave. He swallowed hard, plucking up his courage.

"Do you want to go to the movies this weekend?" he blurted out.

Angela stopped riffling, turned slowly, and gave him a stunned look. "Do you mean you and me?"

"I have my license now," he reminded her nervously. "I thought I could pick you up, maybe we'd get some dinner first . . ."

Angela was still listening, but the expression on her face was far from encouraging. She looked nearly as shocked as if he had just proposed skinny-dipping in the school swimming pool.

"Well—I—I wasn't expecting—" she stammered.

"Unless . . . you don't have a boyfriend, do you?" Ben asked desperately. At least if the rumor was true, if she was really seeing someone, a rejection would be less humiliating.

156

But Angela shook her head. "No. Not really. Just . . . give me a day or two to think about it. All right?"

"All right," he agreed happily, surprised by the sudden positive turn of events. Leaning against her locker for support, he watched as Angela walked off.

She's thinking about it! he told himself jubilantly. *Fantastic!*

Unless she was only thinking of nice ways to tell him no . . .

I'm not going to set myself up for failure, Ben decided, hurrying off to find Mark. *After all, it's a miracle I got this far!*

This is a nightmare, thought Nicole, watching Courtney and Kyle from across the cafeteria on Monday.

At first she had spied surreptitiously, not wanting them to notice. But it hadn't taken her long to realize that she was perfectly safe. Those two were so busy pawing each other, Nicole was pretty sure they hadn't even noticed what was on their trays.

And Nicole wasn't the only one checking them out. All over the cafeteria, heads were turned their way. At first she had tried to convince herself she was paranoid, but unless she was hearing voices, too . . .

No, people are definitely talking about Kyle and Courtney, just like I predicted. And what they were saying wasn't nice.

Just like I predicted.

Nicole watched in an agony of indecision. Should she go over there? Should she ignore them?

Should she pretend she didn't even know what was going on?

That shouldn't be too hard.

Nicole had spotted Jeff earlier, sitting with friends at a table near the wall. She glanced his way again now, just in time to catch him looking at Courtney. His expression was guarded, and Nicole didn't know him well enough to be sure what he was thinking. But one thing seemed pretty clear: He didn't look jealous.

Then, just before the bell was due to ring, Courtney got up from the table. Kissing Kyle full on the mouth, she managed to tear herself away at last, heading for the exit door alone. Nicole was on her feet in a flash. She finally caught up with her friend outside the girls' room in the main hall.

"Courtney! Wait!"

"Hey, Nicole," Courtney said, pushing the door open and walking in. "I didn't see you in the cafeteria."

"I saw you," Nicole replied, with just the right amount of emphasis.

Courtney didn't seem to notice. She shut herself into a stall, carrying on the conversation through the door. "Didn't Kyle look hot today? I could be perfectly happy just sitting and looking at him."

"Good plan. You ought to try it."

"What?"

"He's got a reputation, Court. You know that—you helped spread the rumors."

A toilet flushed.

"Reputation!" Courtney snorted, pushing out of the stall. "Grow up, Nicole. That's so junior high."

Was it? Nicole shifted her weight uncertainly while Courtney washed her hands.

"I don't think so, Courtney. But even if it is, you've got to drop that guy. You're making a fool of yourself."

"Says who?" Courtney's green eyes crackled in the mirror over the sink. She spun around, hands dripping.

"It's just . . . everyone is looking," Nicole pleaded. "People are talking about you."

"Did it ever occur to you that that's exactly what I want?"

"Yes. But I hoped I was wrong."

"Meaning?"

"This isn't going to get him back, Court. If you're trying to make Jeff jealous, you're going about it all wrong."

"Like you're such an expert," Courtney sneered. "What do you know?"

"I know Hope! And if that's the kind of girl he likes, you're giving him the exact opposite. How is that going to help?"

Courtney shook her head. "Stick to what you're good at, Nicole, which *isn't* what guys like. Have you and Mr. Holy even made it to first base?"

Nicole blanched. "This isn't about me."

"No? I think it's *all* about you. You're not afraid of what people will say about me—you're afraid of what they'll say about you."

"I'm trying to help you, Court. That guy is using you!"

Courtney's eyes were cold. "Maybe I'm using him."

"Whatever. Look, Courtney, I don't want to fight. And if you really *liked* Kyle, I'd stand behind you. But if this is just about Jeff . . ."

"Will you shut up about Jeff?" Courtney snapped. "I couldn't care less about Jeff! I *do not care*. Do you get it?"

She slammed out of the bathroom before Nicole could answer, her long coat flapping out behind her.

Yeah, I get it, thought Nicole, temporarily immobilized by the scene. *You don't care about Jeff.*

She rolled her eyes, half wishing she had a witness.

Right. Anyone can see that.

Melanie had barely arrived for Tuesday afternoon's open practice when Nicole ran over to her. Pathetically eager and dressed to perfection, she hovered a few feet away, apparently waiting for the order to split into groups.

There was no questioning Nicole's dedication. She had arrived early at every meeting, always wearing some completely color-coordinated ensemble with matching hair accessories. Tall, rail thin, and perfectly groomed, Nicole had grown up a lot since September. Melanie would even have gone so far as to say she was one of the cuter girls trying out.

If only her body was as coordinated as her outfits.

"Hi, Melanie," Nicole said shyly, sidling up as if they barely knew each other. "I want to get in your group again, because I really like the way you teach us."

Melanie nodded, embarrassed. Was Nicole kissing up to her? Melanie was used to being deferred to, but she hated people sucking up to her. It was so pointless and degrading to everyone involved.

"Okay, people!" Sandra shouted over the growing din of voices in the gym. "Let's get into groups and get going!"

There was a scramble for positions, and Melanie noticed that a few more people had dropped out. Instead of twelve girls per group, now there were more like nine. For only four spots, however, the competition was still fierce.

"All right, people," Melanie addressed her bunch,

sounding exactly like Sandra. "We're going to work on learning the rest of the dance first. We'll practice the cheer after that."

"Can we do the whole dance from the beginning?" a blonde asked anxiously. "I wasn't here last time, and I want to make sure my friend taught me right."

The brunette next to her rolled her eyes, clearly annoyed.

"We're going to run through it from the beginning, but I'm not going to reteach parts you've already learned. You'll just have to get it as you go along."

"I'll help you afterwards with anything you missed," Nicole offered grandly.

That ought to be interesting, Melanie thought.

"Thanks, but I'll be okay," the girl said quickly. Apparently she'd seen Nicole in action.

"All right. We'll do it with the music in a minute, but first we'll just walk through the new steps. Everyone watch me. *One*, two, *three*, four . . ."

Melanie demonstrated as she counted off the music, feeling more self-conscious than she ever had at a game. She knew people were watching her at games, of course—probably *more* people—but she didn't think they studied her like this, dissecting her every move.

"Everyone try it now. I'll go slow. *One*, two . . ."

Melanie watched over her shoulder as she led her

group through the steps a few times. About half of them seemed to pick it up easily. The other half, including Nicole, struggled along, seeming always to have a leftover hand or a foot they didn't know what to do with.

"On your own now," Melanie said. "On my count."

Melanie circled the group as she called the count, trying to give the appearance of impartially checking on everyone. Even so, most of her attention was focused on Nicole.

Long and lean, Nicole had all the elements for a great line. If she would only step out a little more crisply, and snap her arms a little harder . . .

"You need to line up your hands with your arms," Melanie told her, stepping in impulsively. "Look at mine—they're straight lines. When you break your wrists like that, you ruin the whole effect."

Nicole stared at her, speechless. Melanie didn't know what the girl was thinking, but since she'd already gone that far . . .

"And straighten your elbows. Please. That arm should snap into position. Snap!"

Melanie demonstrated, turning her attention back to the whole group as if she'd been talking to everyone all along. Nicole was still staring as if she'd been struck dumb. Only her turquoise eyes showed any sign of life.

She's offended, Melanie thought. *Or else completely*

163

confused. Either way, I should have kept my big mouth shut.

She couldn't risk appearing to have a favorite—especially if that person didn't appreciate her tips.

"All right, let's run through it again. I'll clap the beat this time. Ready? And . . ."

Melanie began clapping, watching the girls move through the steps. She was almost afraid to look at Nicole, but when she did she saw something amazing.

"Again," she called, still clapping.

Nicole had it down! She was practically the best in the group now on that one little section.

What a difference straight arms make!

"One more time. Step *out*, Nicole. Step out like you mean it."

Nicole stepped out, hitting the count perfectly. Melanie watched her, dumbfounded. How could anyone improve so much in only five short minutes?

All she needs is a coach, Melanie realized. *Someone to work with her one-on-one.*

Not that Melanie was likely to volunteer. Nicole didn't even like her. And Sandra had lectured the entire squad about showing favoritism.

But if she managed to find someone else, I think she'd actually have a chance.

Thirteen

"Leah!" someone yelled in the hall Wednesday morning.

Leah turned at her locker, trying to spot who had called her. Peter was working his way over, weaving through the crowd. When their eyes made contact, he waved, as if to make sure she'd wait.

"Hi, Peter," she called, waving back. A moment later he was at her side.

"What are you up to?" she asked. "Your homeroom isn't down this way, is it?"

"No." Peter checked his watch. "But class doesn't start for ten minutes, and I was hoping to talk to you."

"To me?" Something about the request made her nervous. Perhaps it was the slightly desperate expression on his face. "Here?"

He cast his gaze around. "How about in that classroom?" he suggested, pointing to an open doorway. "No one's in there yet."

Leah nodded and followed him inside, her apprehension growing with every step. If all Peter wanted was to say hello or set up an Eight Prime meeting, there was no need for privacy. Sure enough, the moment they were alone, he turned to her with pleading eyes.

"I was wondering . . . I've noticed you and Jenna have been hanging around together lately, and I was hoping you could help me out."

The little hairs on the back of Leah's neck rose. She knew what was coming next.

"Oh?"

"It's just that ever since Sarah's accident, Jenna's been acting strange—quiet, or distracted, or something. Just not herself. I've asked her about it a bunch of times. I asked her again last weekend. But she keeps saying it's nothing."

"Mmm." Leah was afraid to say anything else, for fear she would say it all. She was *dying* to tell Peter what she knew. Keeping the secret was torture, and besides, Jenna just wasn't being fair. True, the fact that he'd kissed Melanie was pretty shocking, but Peter and Jenna weren't even a couple then. It wasn't technically cheating. Leah sympathized with Jenna's insecurities, but the girl was her own worst enemy. How could she win if she refused to compete?

"When this first started," Peter went on, "I asked Melanie if Jenna had said anything to her, or if she had any idea if Jenna might be mad at me. She couldn't think of a reason, though, and neither can I."

Leah felt her eyebrows go up despite her best attempt at a blank expression. So it was true what people said: Denial wasn't just a river in Egypt.

"Really? The two of you couldn't think of *anything?*"

"No. Can you?" Peter asked earnestly. He looked so sweet and pathetic and worried that Leah's heart turned over. It wasn't hard to see why Jenna loved him.

"Well . . ."

The entire story was right on the tip of her tongue. *Someone* had to give the poor guy a clue, and here was the perfect chance.

Except that I promised Jenna I wouldn't.

Except that I'd be helping her if I did.

Leah opened her mouth. Shut it again. Opened it. Shut it.

The need to straighten out the whole silly mess was killing her.

"I . . . I can't think of a thing," she squeaked.

"Huh?"

"I *said,* are you going to eat that roll?" Mark repeated with exaggerated care, as if he were talking to a particularly dense brick wall.

"Oh. You can have it," Ben said. Barely glancing at his friend, he returned his gaze to the cheerleaders' table.

Angela was there, between Melanie and Lou Anne. Her long hair was tied in a high ponytail, spilling glossy brown curls down her back. Her sweater that day was the color of butter. Soft, creamy butter. Ben's hand flexed under the table as he imagined touching it. Not in a crude way—just a brush along the sleeve, or maybe a pat on the shoulder.

"Butter?" Mark asked.

"What?" Ben jumped halfway out of his seat.

"I *said*, can I have your *butter* to go with this *roll*? What is wrong with you today?"

"Huh? Oh. Nothing."

Mark reached across the table and helped himself to Ben's butter. Ben drifted back to Angela.

"Who are you looking at? Angela?"

"What? No!"

"I think you are."

"You want to keep your voice down?" Ben begged.

"It's been two days now. I think you'd better give up."

"She said she'd let me know." Ben grimaced at the realization that he'd just inadvertently admitted he *had* been watching Angela.

"People say a lot of things." The words were cynical, but Mark's voice was not unkind. "So you took a shot. You got farther than I thought you would. Set your sights a little lower next time, and who knows?"

"She said she'd get back to me," Ben repeated stubbornly.

Angela wasn't the type of girl who would make a promise like that, then leave a guy hanging forever. Some girls would. They'd even defend their actions by saying that the fact they'd never answered should have made their answer clear. But not Angela. She was nice.

Ben glanced longingly over his shoulder again, only to see his dream girl rising to her feet. She carried her tray to the trash can, then turned and walked right toward him.

"I think she's coming over!" Mark said with obvious amazement.

"Shhh!" Ben hushed him frantically.

Angela's pants that day were forest green. As she walked her high-heeled boots clicked, just barely audible under the other cafeteria noises. Ben watched in a trance as she approached, taking in the melting brown eyes, flawless olive skin, and little beauty mark by the corner of her mouth.

She was perfect. Perfect! If he'd had all the power in the world, Ben wouldn't have changed a thing. On the contrary, every time he saw her he felt like writing fan mail to God.

"Hello, Ben," she said softly.

"Hi, Angela!" he brayed, wincing at his own lack of finesse.

She glanced around the table where he was sitting. He and Mark were on an end, with a little space between them and the next guys, but things were still fairly crowded. Leaning down to his ear, she cupped a hand around her mouth. His nose caught just a hint of some light perfume before she tore his dreams apart.

"I'm sorry, Ben," she whispered. "I just don't think it would be a good idea."

He tried to speak, to argue his case, but he couldn't find even one word.

"It was sweet of you to ask, though. Thanks."

She smiled at him before she walked off, a flash of perfect white teeth. This time her clicking heels sounded like nails pounding into his coffin.

"I guess she said no, huh?" Mark asked sympathetically.

Ben didn't need to ask how his friend had guessed. He was sure the bad news was all over his face.

"At least she did it nicely. Whispering and all. She could have made it a lot more embarrassing."

Ben nodded miserably, unable to speak past the enormous lump in his throat.

"It was a long shot from the start," his friend reminded him gently. "You knew that."

Maybe he'd known it once, but somehow in the past two weeks Ben had convinced himself that he actually had a chance. The idea seemed laughable now. So why, as he stared down at the spaghetti blurring on his tray, had he never felt less like laughing? In fact, if there hadn't been such a big crowd . . .

"You're not going to start crying, are you?" Mark asked, alarmed.

Ben shook his head. "I have to go," he blurted out, lurching to his feet. "There's, uh . . . something under my contacts."

He ran for the bathroom, not really caring if his friend had believed him or not. Besides, there *was* something under his contacts: a flood of unshed tears that threatened to float them right out. The last thing Ben needed now was to be seen crying in the cafeteria.

Assuming it was possible for his social standing to fall any lower, that would definitely do the trick.

"Am I allowed to park here?" Miguel wondered. There were a bunch of open spots in the CU parking lot he had entered, but a confusing sign at its entrance had said something about student and faculty parking in marked spaces only. As far as he could tell, the space in front of him wasn't marked. Did that mean it was free?

"Here goes nothing," he said nervously, guiding his car between the lines. After all, if he couldn't even figure out how to *park* at college, there wasn't much hope for the rest of his academic career. Besides, it was nearly four o'clock on a Wednesday. CCHS was a ghost town that late in the day, so how many students could still want to park at CU?

"It'll be fine," he said firmly, more to reassure himself than because he believed it. Lifting his completed application off the passenger seat, he climbed out and slammed his car door. The nearby buildings of the college loomed, outlined against a gray sky. Taking a deep breath, Miguel set off toward them with long, determined strides.

He could have just put his application in the mail. That certainly would have been easier, but he'd already lost so much time. Now that he'd made up his mind to go to CU, Miguel was excited enough about the decision that he wanted to save a day or two by delivering his paperwork in person. He wasn't sure that would increase his chances of being accepted, but it definitely couldn't hurt.

Now all I have to do is find the registrar's office, he thought, wishing he'd let Leah give him a map of the campus after all. Even though she had once hoped he would follow her to a more prestigious college, she'd been thrilled enough by the prospect of his finally applying anywhere to offer to draw him a map on the spot—complete with directions to her parents' offices in case he had any trouble. Miguel had not only declined, however; he had scoffed at the idea that he might need help to find his way around a school.

I just didn't expect it to be quite so big.

At the edge of the parking lot, Miguel stepped up to concrete and wandered through some buildings he took to be dorms—only to find more concrete and buildings on their other side. It seemed there was nothing but concrete and buildings as far as the eye could see, with only a few scattered trees and small squares of lawn. He had driven the perimeter of the school before picking a place to park, but this new sense of how large the place was slightly overwhelmed him, especially since the campus was anything but the ghost town he'd predicted.

People were everywhere; on foot, on bikes, or on skateboards. They seemed to head in ten directions at once, except for the packs who were just hanging out, congregating by every bench and tree. And nowhere did Miguel see a teacher, or anyone who even looked like one. It was as if the entire place were being run by students, and although many of them weren't much older than CCHS seniors, they had an entirely different look about them—like people in charge of their own destinies. A sense of purpose pervaded the atmosphere.

Miguel liked the place right away.

At a corner by a sign that read LOCKSLEY HALL, Miguel stopped a guy walking in the opposite direction.

"Excuse me. Can you tell me where the registrar's office is?"

"New, huh?" the guy said with a smile. "Finding your way around here is a nightmare at first, but you'll get used to it."

Pointing diagonally across more concrete to more buildings, he rattled off a series of left and right turns that left Miguel's head spinning. The guy laughed, reading his expression. "Just go as far as you can, then ask someone else. We've all been through the same thing."

"All right. Thanks."

Miguel took off in the indicated direction, head held high so as not to look lost. Soon he began crossing a wide, open square, like the quad back at CCHS but much larger. The view opened out on all sides, making the campus seem less packed and paved over. Now there were lots of trees, and a lush expanse of rolling lawn. On his right, a fountain gurgled noisily. He could imagine the scene in warm weather, with people sprawled out on the grass and girls in summer dresses every way a person looked. Not that he'd be *looking*.

Not like that, anyway.

Miguel had to ask directions twice more before he found the registrar's office. The building was just about to close as he skidded in through the front door. A woman at the counter took his application, placing the envelope, unopened, into a bin behind her.

"Do you think I'll get in?" he asked.

She chuckled. "Now, honey, how would I know that?"

"Well, I mean, is there room? Or have they picked everyone already?"

"Freshman admissions are still open, if that's what you mean. There's room for the right people."

A grin grabbed Miguel's face. "Thanks. Thanks a lot!"

He pushed back out through the door, still smiling, feeling like he'd accomplished something fantastic. He'd be let in—he was sure of it now. And as he strode back across the campus he felt a swelling pride in his new school.

For the first time in his life, he could truly see himself going there. And not just going there but liking it. Liking it a lot.

He picked up the pace, his grin growing with each step.

This is my dream. I'm going to be a doctor. And CU is where I'm going to start.

Fourteen

"Dad?" Melanie said cautiously, creeping into the downstairs den after school on Thursday.

Her father was sprawled on the sofa, an old movie turned down to a nearly inaudible level on the television before him. For a moment she thought he'd fallen asleep in the darkened room, but then he raised his head a fraction.

"Mel? You hava good day?"

There was just enough of a slur to his words to match the six-pack of empty beer cans around him. From experience, Melanie knew that her father was almost fully functional at this stage, although he was far less likely to remember things the next day— especially if he kept drinking. She had stumbled onto the perfect moment to put her new plan into action.

"It was okay," she answered, wandering farther into the room. "Dad, could you open up the safe?"

"Huh?" He roused himself into a sitting position. "What for?"

"Mom had a necklace I want to wear. Not one of the fancy ones," she added quickly, at the sight of the face he made. "It was just a silver chain with a little silver sun. Remember?"

"I'm not sure."

She had hoped for an answer like that. She had purposely chosen something inexpensive and without special meaning, knowing how stubborn he got about the pieces that had a strong association with her mother. The jewelry Tristyn had worn and the paintings she had made were all that was left of her now, and her husband protected them fiercely, as he hadn't been able to protect her life.

"So can I wear it?"

"I guess so," he said, not moving. "You'll get them all someday, you know."

He stared over the top of the television set, lost in thought. The movie played on, unheeded. Melanie stood waiting, shifting her weight back and forth.

"Dad?"

"Huh?" he said, startled.

"Could you get it for me, please?"

"Oh. Right."

He rose from the sofa with just the slightest trace of unsteadiness and tightened the sash on his bathrobe. Shuffling past her in his old slippers, he led the way up the stairs.

"I haven't had that thing open in a couple of years. I hope I remember the combination," he said as they walked into the library.

177

The comment took Melanie by surprise. Was there any real chance he didn't? What would she do then?

"I, uh, I hope so too," she managed to get out.

Her father removed the false panel from the book-case, expressing surprise that it came off so easily. "I thought it might be stuck after all this time. . . . That thing came off like I was just in here a couple of days ago."

Melanie hovered behind him, grateful that he couldn't see her face.

"Let me think," he said, squatting in front of the safe. He rocked back and forth on his heels a few seconds, then reached for the combination dial and began spinning it to the left. Melanie tried to watch over his shoulder without being obvious, but his head kept dipping into the way. She didn't see how many turns of the dial he made before he finally stopped on 24.

A lot, she told herself. *A lot to the left, end on 24.*

He was already spinning back to the right, hitting a number there and reversing to the left.

It looked like maybe 9, she thought anxiously, her heart starting to pound. *Was it three times around?* He was going way too fast—and how many times could she ask him to demonstrate before he finally caught on to her plan?

He stopped his spinning at what might have been 88 and reversed again. All of a sudden, the dial seemed to stop on its own. He reached for the T-shaped

178

handle and turned it ninety degrees, pulling the big door open.

That's the combination? 24-9-88-stop? No wonder I couldn't guess it! Those are totally random numbers! She worked to commit them to memory, looking forward to the moment she could run to her room and write them down.

"Okay, so let's see about that necklace," he said.

Her father's body almost completely blocked her view into the open safe. Melanie leaned forward to peer over his shoulder, catching a glimpse of row upon row of large and small jewelry boxes.

"If it was inexpensive, it's probably in one of these big boxes," her father said, lifting out the most accessible one. Turning to his left, he set it on the floor and opened the hinged lid. Inside, dividers partitioned the space into numerous square compartments, each one holding a piece of silver jewelry. "Hey, this looks like a good place to start, Mel."

"Uh-huh."

Her father began poking through the jewelry, but Melanie barely glanced at it in her eagerness to learn what else was in the safe. She cocked her head to see farther inside, catching her breath at the sight of some old manila envelopes. They were shoved off to the right wall, almost invisible behind the jewelry boxes, but even with her current lousy view, Melanie could see they were stuffed with papers.

"You know, Dad, it could take a long time to find

that necklace. If you don't want to hang around, I'll look for it myself and call you when it's time to—"

"Got it!" Mr. Andrews said triumphantly, lifting a silver chain by one finger. It swung and sparkled in the late-afternoon rays slanting through the library windows, the little silver sun glowing as if with a light of its own. "Now what were the odds of that? The very first box!"

Yeah, thought Melanie, stifling a groan. *What were the odds?*

Handing her the necklace, he shut the lid on the jewelry box, put it back in place, and closed the safe door, spinning the dial over and over to make sure it was locked. He replaced the panel, then stood up to face her. "Well?"

She didn't know what he wanted. "Um, thanks?"

"You're welcome, but that's not what I meant. Aren't you going to put it on?"

The sun dangled from her hand. She glanced down as if seeing it for the first time. "Yes. I was just going to, uh—"

"Here. I'll help you." Mr. Andrews took the necklace and opened the clasp on the chain. "Turn around."

She turned obediently, standing like a statue while he fastened it around her neck.

"There. You'll have to fix your hair. Let me see."

Melanie turned slowly, using both hands to

lift her hair from beneath the chain. The pendant settled into position low on her neck. Her father smiled.

"You look just like her, you know. She was beautiful. And you're growing up beautiful too. I'm so proud of you, Mel."

"You are?" The words fell from her in her surprise.

"Of course. You're your mother's daughter, and you're a good girl. Someday you and I'll sit down and have a long talk."

"About?"

He waved a distracted hand. "Things. Life. There's no hurry. Besides, aren't you going to that meeting?"

Melanie glanced at the clock. There was an Eight Prime meeting at Peter's house later that night. "Not for a while."

"Got a ride to that?"

"Peter's coming for me."

"That's good." He smiled again, a little sadly this time. "Like I said, you're a good girl."

He shuffled out of the room, leaving her stunned behind him. What had he been rambling about? And why pick now to praise her, when she was breaking his trust right and left?

Because he doesn't know I am.

For a moment, she felt horribly guilty. She loved her father; she didn't want to deceive him. But she also didn't want to invite him back into a past that had hurt them so much. What if he didn't know about the stuff she was learning? Or, if he did, what if he got mad at her for digging it up again?

It's better this way, she thought sadly, her eyes still focused on the place where his back had disappeared. She took a few deep breaths, shoving down her doubts.

And then she ran for her room.

24-9-88-stop. 24-9-88-stop. 24-9-88-stop. Oh, for Pete's sake! Where did I put all my pencils?

"Are you guys ready?" Peter looked around his living room, waiting for the members of Eight Prime to stop talking. "We have a lot to do tonight."

Everyone was already seated around the coffee table. Leah, Miguel, and Ben had the sofa, Jesse the big armchair. Melanie sat beside Peter on the love seat, while Jenna and Nicole had dining room chairs brought in for the occasion. Peter snuck a glance at Jenna, hurt that she had chosen to sit there instead of next to him, but he could hardly make a fuss in front of their friends.

"I didn't get a treasury report," Ben complained. "I don't even know what we're supposed to be talking about."

Miguel set his Coke on the table and handed Ben a paper from the stack in front of them. "Here you go, Sherlock. They were pretty hard to find."

Ben grabbed the paper, shooting Miguel a surprisingly crabby look. Nicole giggled, then froze at the icy glance Ben turned her way.

Jenna flipped open her steno pad.

"Does everyone have a report now?" Peter paused. "Then you can see that between the Valentine's Day sale and the sucker sale, we did pretty well."

"I think you made a mistake adding up these numbers," Leah said. "This can't be right."

"No, that's how much we have. Everyone's been paid back, and that's the balance in our passbook."

"It's too much," Leah insisted.

"I put in a little extra," Peter confessed.

"You didn't have to do that, Peter!" Melanie reproached him.

"I wanted to," he said quickly. "No big deal. What we need to talk about tonight is how we're going to earn the rest of the money we'll need for the Junior Explorers' day camp."

"Do you know how much that is?" Nicole asked.

"Not exactly," he admitted. "But a lot more than we have."

"It's almost warm enough to wash cars again," Melanie proposed.

Jenna shot her a hostile look before she wrote the suggestion down. "I don't want to wash cars," she said.

"We've already done everything there is," said Nicole. "I'm fund-raisered out."

"What do you mean by that?" Peter asked uneasily. "You don't want to help?"

"No, I'll help. I just can't think of anything to do."

"Why does it have to be a fund-raiser?" Jesse asked, reclining lazily in the armchair. "I've got a better idea."

"You do?"

Everyone looked in Jesse's direction.

"We're all ears," Leah said.

Jesse took his time, apparently enjoying the attention. He sat up straight and then leaned forward slightly, letting the suspense build.

"Instead of a fund-raiser, why not have a work party out at the camp? We can put a notice in the paper, inviting the whole town to come out on some certain day to help clean up and build things. Not only that, but we'll ask them to bring whatever building materials they can donate."

"Go on," Peter urged, excited by the idea.

"Sure. Everyone's garage is half stuffed with left-over junk from working on their houses anyway. Someone brings half a sheet of plywood, someone else brings the old faucets that used to be in their bathroom . . . The next thing you know, you have a ton of good stuff for free. *And* the people to install it."

"That's genius!" Peter declared.

Jesse smiled. "I know."

"We had a ton of volunteers working on the haunted house, and that went really well," Leah said in support.

"The haunted house was *my* idea," Ben reminded them.

"It sounds great to me," said Miguel. "I'd much rather spend my time building something than standing around trying to sell stuff."

"I'll write the ad for the newspaper," Melanie volunteered. "I have an idea too. What if we put something like 'Cash donations for gas, snacks, art supplies, etc., also gratefully accepted'? We could have a collection jar up at the lake and maybe kill two birds with one stone."

"That's a great idea!" said Nicole. "Some people will put in money, and others might give us paints or Kool-Aid and stuff."

"Maybe a gas station will offer us a discount," said Leah.

"Wouldn't that be great?" Peter said dreamily. Visions of cheap gas floated through his head while the others got louder and louder, all trying to improve on Jesse's idea.

Unfortunately, however, thinking of gas soon made Peter think of taking the bus to a gas station—an impossibility without a driver. How were they going to get by without Chris? Peter opened his mouth to ask the group for ideas on that but changed his mind at the last second. He was determined to find a solution, so why bring everyone down when they were all so excited?

"When should we do it?" he asked instead.

A heated debate followed. Everyone agreed it should be sometime during the upcoming spring break. But which day?

"How about this Saturday?" Melanie proposed. "It's better to do it right away, because if we wait too long, people might be out of town on vacation."

"Too soon," said Jesse. "That only gives us tomorrow to get the word out."

"Sunday, then," she said. "That's the paper everyone reads anyway."

"No good," Miguel said flatly. "Palm Sunday."

"Both Sundays are out," Jenna said, "because Easter comes after that."

"Since everyone's out of school, we could do it during the week," said Nicole.

Jesse shook his head. "Bad idea. We want all those working adults to come out with their power tools. Oh!" He pointed to Melanie. "Put that in the ad. Bring tools."

"Next Saturday, then," said Peter. "It's all that's left."

"We should still run the ad this Sunday," Melanie insisted.

"We'll run it on Sunday, and again next Friday. That ought to get a response."

"I hope it doesn't rain," Ben said dourly.

The big issues settled, people got out of their seats, ready to leave.

"Hey, Melanie, do you need a ride?" Nicole offered. "I can drive you home if you want."

Say yes, Peter willed silently. If he didn't have to drive Melanie, perhaps he could convince Jenna to stay awhile after everyone else left.

"Uh, all right. Thanks."

The two girls left behind Ben, who barely grunted good-bye before beating everyone out the door. He was definitely in a bad mood about something that night, but Peter didn't have time to ask why.

He had problems of his own.

Grabbing the seat Nicole had just vacated, Peter leaned over to see the meeting notes Jenna was finishing up. She slammed the steno pad shut.

"All done!" Reaching under her chair for her backpack, she began zipping the notes away.

"What are you doing after this?" Peter asked her. "You want to hang out and watch TV or something? I still have those ice cream bonbons."

"I can't," she said, jumping to her feet. "It's getting late, and I want to stop by the hospital on my way home."

"The hospital! Won't Sarah already be asleep?"

"Maybe. Maybe not. Either way, I promised I'd say goodnight."

"Could you call her?"

187

"No."

"I'm taking off, Peter," Jesse called from the door. "See you at school tomorrow."

Peter waved distractedly, trailing Jenna across the living room. "Are you sure?"

"I'm positive. I'll see you tomorrow, too."

Opening the door Jesse had just shut, she stalked out into the night, leaving Leah and Miguel standing behind her at the exit. Peter turned to Leah.

"Do you see what I'm talking about?" he demanded. "What was that?"

Leah just gave him a helpless look. "Why don't you ask her tomorrow?"

"Tomorrow!" Peter spat as he shut the door behind them. "Tomorrow. I'm *sick* of tomorrow. It's always a day away."

"So. Good meeting," said Nicole, trying not to show how nervous she was as she drove to Melanie's house.

"Pretty good." Melanie fiddled with the necklace she was wearing, running the charm back and forth on its chain. "It looks like I'll be up late, though. If I'm going to call that ad in tomorrow morning, I'll have to write it tonight."

"I can help you!" Nicole offered eagerly. Too eagerly.

Melanie stopped fiddling to give her a penetrating look.

"I mean, uh, if you want me to," Nicole amended, trying not to flinch.

"That's all right."

Melanie dropped the necklace back to her chest. Silence descended in the car.

You're just going to have to ask her, Nicole thought anxiously. *This is the best chance you'll ever get*.

And it hadn't been accidental. Throughout the entire Eight Prime meeting, Nicole had been poised on the edge of her seat, determined to be the first to offer Melanie a ride. The moment things had been settled she'd spoken up, before Jesse or Peter could get the idea.

"So. Um. No cheerleading practice for a long time," Nicole said, turning a corner. "I wish they were holding practice during spring break. We could practice every day."

Melanie looked at her as if she were out of her mind. "Not even Sandra is that gung-ho. Why would you want to waste your whole vacation practicing?"

"It wouldn't be a waste! I really want to make the squad. And . . . well . . . I could use the extra work."

Melanie nodded slightly. The barest gesture, but Nicole knew what it meant: Without a miracle, her dream was dead.

"Would you coach me next week?" she blurted out. "It doesn't have to be every day. Just when you can. Even once would help. Or if you could just give me some tips about that original dance we're supposed to make up. I'm no choreographer. I don't know how to pick out the music or make up the steps or . . ."

She trailed off uneasily. Melanie was studying her with flat green eyes, her expression completely detached. Her shoulders moved in a small circle; then she sighed.

"Everyone's supposed to practice on their own," she said coolly. "If I coach you, doesn't that give you an unfair advantage?"

Nicole recoiled as if slapped.

I should have known she wouldn't say yes! she thought furiously, barely able to concentrate on driving. *I thought she'd changed, but she hasn't! She's still the snobbiest, most stuck-up, most conceited, most—*

"On the other hand," Melanie said slowly, "I know Tiffany and Vanessa are both coaching people, and Sandra never actually said we *couldn't* . . ."

Nicole gasped as Melanie's meaning sunk in. "You'll do it, then? You'll coach me?"

"Why not? I'm not doing anything next week."

"Oh!" Nicole gave up on trying to drive, pulling to the side of the road instead.

"I *love* you!" she cried, throwing her arms around Melanie's neck. "I'm sure to make the squad now!"

"All right," Melanie said calmly, removing Nicole's choke hold using just her fingertips. "Let's not get carried away. And I don't think we ought to tell anyone, either. No point making a big deal about it."

"Sure. Absolutely. Whatever you say," Nicole babbled gratefully. "I'll owe you for this for the rest of my life."

"That seems like a little too long. You don't even know if I'll be any help."

"You're too modest," Nicole protested, deliriously happy.

With a coach like Melanie, how could she lose?

Fifteen

From the desk of Principal Kelly
(Teachers: Please read in homeroom.)

Good morning, students!

As everyone knows, spring break begins tomorrow. I am confident, however, that the impending vacation will not distract any of you diligent people from today's important classwork.

The two months of school remaining after the break are always packed with activities. Let me take this opportunity to mention two. Cheerleaders will be selected after final tryouts on April 15. The Junior & Senior Prom will be held in the ballroom of the Lakehouse Lodge on Saturday, April 24. Start planning ahead for these final, fun-packed weeks before graduation.

Also, don't forget Principal Appreciation Day on April 21—a CCHS tradition, and my personal favorite.

Have a great vacation!

Go, Wildcats!

The main hall was a circus, a milling, screaming mob of just-dismissed students with a whole week of freedom before them. They ran, slammed locker doors, and literally bounced off the walls in their eagerness to be gone. Leah strode through the chaos in search of Peter.

The night before, after the Eight Prime meeting, she had tossed and turned for hours, worrying and wondering what the right thing to do was. She had awoken as undecided as she'd gone to bed, and nearly as tired. It wasn't until fifth period that afternoon that Leah had finally come to a conclusion: She had to tell Peter what she knew about Jenna. If she did it now, before the vacation, the two of them would have a whole week to make up and get things back to normal. Besides, if she didn't do it now, she'd almost surely talk herself out of it again.

"Peter!" she shouted, spotting him by a side exit door. "Peter!"

He turned and waved, and a moment later she was at his side, following him through the crowded exit and down the broad outside stairs. The afternoon was cool but sunny, promising warmer days to come.

"I want to talk to you about last night," Leah said, the moment people had spread out enough to ensure them some privacy. She turned toward the student parking lot, but Peter stopped and pointed in the other direction, toward the gym.

"I'm on my bike," he explained.

"Oh. Well, I guess we can talk here." She glanced around to make sure no one was listening. "What I wanted to say is, I think I know why Jenna was so cold last night."

"You do?" Peter asked hopefully.

Leah nodded. "She was upset that you brought Melanie."

"What? What for? Melanie always comes to Eight Prime meetings."

"Yes, but you don't always drive her."

"What difference does it make? She needed a ride. I'm sorry, Leah, but I think you're way off base."

"I'm not." Her eyes held his, trying to convey her certainty. "I know I'm not."

"It doesn't make any sense," Peter insisted.

"It does to Jenna." Leah glanced around again, then pulled him a little farther from the building, over to a tree. "It would to me, too, if I were her."

"I don't get it."

"She's *jealous*, Peter! She told me you kissed Melanie, and it's tearing her up inside. *That's* what this whole thing's about. All of it."

The color drained from Peter's cheeks. "That was one time. It was . . . I already apologized."

Leah nodded. "And personally I think she ought to accept that. I think *she* thinks she ought to accept it. But the whole situation has made her really insecure. She's angry at Melanie, she feels awkward around you—she just doesn't know what to do."

"Here's a suggestion: How about get over it?" His eyes flashed as he ground out the words.

Leah took a step backward, amazed. Peter was always so calm, so easygoing. Nothing ever seemed to bother him. There was no mistaking his current mood, though.

Peter was angry. *Really* angry.

"I shouldn't have said anything," she moaned, wishing desperately that she hadn't. "I was only trying to help. I thought that if you knew what Jenna was upset about, you could apologize and—"

"I already apologized! And she has no right to be mad. It's not like she was pining over me when it happened. Not hardly! In fact, she was totally obsessed with—"

He shook his head, as if to clear the angry thoughts, but the next words out of his mouth were just as furious. "You know what? *She* ought to apologize to *me*! She lied to me, Leah. She's been lying for weeks."

"I shouldn't have said anything," Leah repeated in a panic. "Jenna told me not to. I only thought that—"

"Oh, sure. Don't *tell* me!" Peter sneered. "That would take all the fun out of torturing the clueless guy."

He stood there a moment, arms stiff at his sides, ready to explode.

"I have to go." Turning abruptly, he stalked off toward the gym.

"Don't be mad," Leah called after him. He never turned around.

What an idiot I am! she thought, covering her face with her hands. *What have I done?*

She'd only been trying to patch things up between two good friends—instead she had made them worse. *I just never expected him to react like that. Peter's always so reasonable. I didn't see that coming.*

And then a new fear gripped her: *What if he tells Jenna?*

She sat down hard in the wet grass, unable to stop a sudden rush of guilty tears. *Of course he's going to tell Jenna. And even if Jenna forgives him now, she'll never forgive me.*

Leah buried her face in her arms. *I wouldn't forgive me either.*

Ben didn't move when the telephone rang. For one thing, it was never for him. Besides, he was too busy sulking on the sofa, pretending to watch TV.

Friday night. The first night of spring break. Everyone in the world has plans tonight. Or at least a friend to hang out with.

Everyone but him, of course, and maybe one or two other losers.

Yep, getting my driver's license really changed everything. I'm Mr. Popular now.

"Benny! It's for you!" his mother called from upstairs.

Probably Mark. Except that even Mark was going out to dinner with his family. *Maybe they haven't left yet.*

With a sigh, Ben heaved himself out of the dented cushions and walked to the phone in the kitchen. "Hello?"

"Ben? Hi, it's Angela. I hope you don't mind my calling—I found your number in the book."

"Angela?"

"I've been thinking. . . . and I was wondering if you might still want to go to a movie tonight." She hesitated. "If you're not doing something else."

"A movie?" Grabbing his earlobe, he twisted until it hurt. He was definitely awake.

"Yes, but it's not a date," she said quickly. "We can only go together if we agree it's just as friends."

Friends, he thought unhappily. *I should have known.*

Still, it was better than nothing. The more he thought about it, in fact, the more better than nothing it was. He was going to spend an evening with the prettiest girl at school. He'd be out of the house; he'd have fun. And the pressure would definitely be off, since Angela had made it clear that things couldn't go any farther. Finally, and perhaps best of all, people were bound to see them together. Lots of people.

How much of a loser could he be if Angela Maldonado was his friend?

"I'll drive," he volunteered.

"I'll meet you there," she countered. "The show starts in thirty minutes at the mall multiplex."

"Thirty minutes! We have to hurry!"

Angela laughed. "I know. Meet me by the ticket office."

Ben hung up the phone. "Mom! Mom, I'm going to the movies!" he shouted, charging up the stairs to his room. Luckily he had showered before dinner. Now if he could just find some shoes, and maybe a nicer shirt . . .

"You're going on a date?" his mother asked, appearing in his doorway. "With that girl?"

"Not exactly. We're just friends."

Mrs. Pipkin smiled. "You have to start somewhere. Take a twenty from my purse, and you can drive your father's car if you promise to be careful."

"I'll be careful!" Ben promised, nearly breaking his neck in his mad rush back down the stairs.

Outside the theater, Angela was already waiting. She stood to one side of the ticket line, wrapped in a long ivory coat. Her curls spilled over her collar, dark against the light. For a moment, Ben's breath caught in his chest.

Then he rushed forward to meet her, chanting his new mantra: *just friends, just friends, just friends*.

"Hi, Angela."

She smiled, a little shyly. "Hi, Ben. I already got the tickets, so we should probably go right in."

"You didn't buy my ticket, did you? I thought we were going Dutch."

"You can buy the popcorn."

Inside the lobby, Ben bought not just popcorn but two sodas and more candy than two people could possibly eat. He juggled the tub and boxes, praying he wouldn't drop anything, as Angela led the way into the theater. At least she had taken the sodas.

The plush red seats of the theater were only about half full. "How about over there?" Angela suggested, pointing.

"Good. Anywhere," Ben answered, desperate to put down his load. He tried to focus on where he was walking instead of on identifying people from school as he and Angela scooted sideways down the aisle, but he couldn't help smiling proudly at a few blatantly curious faces.

"Here," she decided, sitting down.

Ben took the seat beside her, gratefully dumping all the candy and hardly any popcorn into her lap. Angela laughed as she flicked off the renegade kernels.

"You don't seriously believe I'm going to eat this much candy?"

"You never know. Is this a long movie?"

"You don't even know what we're seeing yet!" she realized. "You really *are* a friend, to go along with this."

Ben smiled, managing not to say that he'd have watched a blank wall if it meant sitting next to her.

Angela reached into the popcorn tub and ate a handful piece by piece. The lights were at that half-dim stage, and there was no one in the seats right around them. The scene was romantic enough that if they *had* been on a date, Ben would have been a nervous wreck.

"You know," she said thoughtfully, turning to him, "my mom says there's a point toward the end of college where all the guys who seemed too quiet and, uh . . . academic in high school become the ones that all the girls want. Suddenly everyone realizes how nice they are."

She hesitated, pushing her hair back off her forehead. "But I guess we're still in high school, aren't we?"

"We sure are," Ben agreed miserably.

Angela just smiled and poked him in the shoulder. "Wait till the ten-year reunion."

Melanie's fingers were stiff with fear as she turned the combination on the library safe. She had already made a couple of attempts, missing the numbers she needed or going around too many times. This time, however, as she turned the dial in the final direction, it seemed to stick on something, coming to rest on its own.

"Let this be it," she begged softly, reaching for the handle. Her father was passed out downstairs; she knew she was crazy not to wait for a safer opportunity. But it was late, and he'd been out of commission long enough that she expected he'd sleep through the night on the sofa.

If alcohol's as good as sleeping pills, he ought to sleep for a week.

The handle turned. The safe was open! Melanie's heart pounded like thunder as she reached behind the jewelry boxes, her fingers closing on the envelopes. She sucked in a deep breath, held it, and pulled the yellowed old things out into the light.

The paper of the envelopes was worn and disintegrated around the edges. One looked as if a mouse had chewed its corners. Melanie sat down on the floor and spread them out before her, trying to decide where to start. There were eleven in all, varying in thickness from nearly flat to completely stuffed.

The fattest one, she decided. Careful not to tear the paper, she unbent the metal clasp and released the unsealed flap.

Inside were stock certificates, official-looking papers with swirly backgrounds saying Mr. Andrews owned so many shares of such and such stock. Melanie paged through them, careful to keep them in order as she looked for something more interesting.

Come on, she thought anxiously, trying to hurry. She didn't want to miss anything, but the whole stack seemed to be financial papers. Flipping through the final pages, she slipped them all back into the envelope and set that one aside.

The next one was full of bills of sale for the cars her parents had collected. The third, receipts for her mother's jewelry.

As Melanie pulled the mismatched papers out of the fourth envelope, something fell from between the pages and dropped to the floor. She stared down at a tiny envelope, like the one from a florist's card, with a single word scrawled on its front: Angel.

"What's that?" she said aloud.

Setting the papers aside, Melanie reached for the card instead. As soon as she picked it up, though, she felt not a card but a small, hard lump inside the paper. The flap had been licked and sealed, but the glue was brittle with age, popping open in her hands. She peeked inside and gasped.

I don't believe it!

Carefully, with two fingertips, she reached inside, drawing out the tarnished silver chain until its large, heart-shaped garnet swung free. It was the necklace she had read about in her mother's diary, the one Trent had given Tristyn when they were seniors in high school. *What is it doing here?*

She had to be getting closer.

Putting the necklace down, Melanie turned

her attention back to the stack of papers. The first thick, stapled document was some kind of trust. Melanie saw her mother's and father's names but didn't understand what it all meant. She set it aside. A similar-looking document bore only her father's name. Under that was another manila envelope, smaller than the one that had contained it. There was one word written across the front of that, too: *Trent*.

"Bingo," Melanie breathed. She nearly ripped the flap open, so close to the secret now. Inside was a marriage license and another thick set of papers. Divorce documents.

"She did it!" Melanie was so shocked she forgot to keep her voice down. "I can't believe she did it!"

But here was the proof in black and white. Tristyn Allen and Trent Wheeler had been joined in holy matrimony by a justice of the peace at Clearwater Crossing City Hall. Melanie compared the date on the marriage license against the date of the divorce. They hadn't even made it two years.

What a disaster. No wonder Mom never talked about it.

Still, it seemed like something she could at least have mentioned. They didn't have to go into every detail, but Melanie felt she had a right to know. She was still clutching those two documents, still reeling, when something else occurred to her.

My parents' marriage license ought to be in here somewhere too, she thought, suddenly wanting very much to see it. Finding out about Trent had completely disrupted her sense of history. The things she had always taken for granted looked different now, with this ugly new fact shoved into the lineup. She wanted to see something that would reinforce what she'd already always believed.

Shuffling through the remaining papers, Melanie came upon the license quickly. She traced her parents' familiar signatures and tried to decipher the faded names of their witnesses. Her parents, too, had been married by a justice of the peace, although their wedding had been held outside.

Beneath the wedding license was her mother's birth certificate. Then her father's. Then hers.

Then another.

"*Four?* Is one a copy or something?"

But something told her it wasn't. Feeling dizzy, she pulled the last one out of the stack.

And then the sound of the library door crashing open made her drop it in terror. Her father supported himself in the door frame, his anger making him larger than life.

"Wha' the heller you doing?" he shouted furiously. "Who told you you're allowed in the safe?"

"See you next week," Howard told Miguel, stopping in the hallway to speak through the open door of the nurses' lounge.

"I might be here over the weekend."

Howard grinned. "I won't."

He waved and walked off as Miguel returned to his paperwork, almost too tired to concentrate.

He had stayed extra late that Friday night, wanting to know what went on after the kids went to sleep. Not much, as it turned out. The nurses still monitored them regularly. There were glasses of water demanded and multiple trips to the bathroom. A couple of the kids had had trouble dropping off, but eventually all was quiet.

At eleven o'clock, one of the nurses had told him to go home. "Unless we get a new patient, or have some type of emergency, this is how it'll be all night. You've seen it all."

Miguel had nodded, worn out. A seven-hour shift after a full day of school had used up his last bit of energy, especially since Zach had had such a rough afternoon. That day's chemotherapy had played havoc with his gut.

"Why don't they just operate?" he'd asked Miguel tearfully between bouts of vomiting. "I want this over with."

"Soon," Miguel had promised, stroking the boy's back and trying not to choke up himself. "The doctors know what they're doing."

At least I hope to God they do, he thought now, staring blankly at the paper in front of him.

The only thing he had to do before he left was

fill out his hours for the week and write a description of what he had done, but he couldn't seem to hold his thoughts together long enough to compose sentences. Finally he managed to jot down something about assisting Howard and the other nurses.

Rising from the table, Miguel dropped his time sheet into the appropriate tray, then slipped his scrub smock off over his head, folding it carefully. He would never have admitted how much he loved wearing it, especially since at this point in his life it was more like playing dress-up than anything else, but that smock made him feel like a doctor. It had a mystique—power, even. He pulled his backpack out of his cubbyhole and started to replace it with the smock, then decided to take both things home.

I might as well do some laundry.

He was still fiddling with his backpack zippers when a flurry of buzzers went off, followed by pages over the loudspeakers and the sound of running feet.

"Code blue, Two West. Code blue, Two West."

Miguel froze. One of the children was in cardiac arrest.

The pediatric resident and a couple of nurses rushed by the open doorway. A red crash cart flew past.

And suddenly Miguel realized where everyone was heading.

Oh, no, he prayed, dropping everything to scramble after them. *God, no. Not Zach. Please, God. Not Zach!*

Find out what happens next in Clearwater Crossing #14, *Love Hurts.*

Laura Peyton Roberts is the author of numerous books for young readers, including all the titles in the Clearwater Crossing series. She holds degrees in both English and geology from San Diego State University. A native Californian, Laura lives in San Diego with her husband and two dogs.

Love Hurts

Every time Jenna sees Melanie, all she can think about is the kiss her friend shared with Peter. Jenna wants to believe it meant nothing, but her jealous heart tells her that's not true. Maybe she and Peter never should have turned their friendship into romance. And maybe breaking up would be the best thing for them all. . . .

Miguel loves volunteering at the hospital. Not only does he witness the incredible work of the doctors firsthand, he's making a difference in the lives of sick kids, especially nine-year-old Zach. The nurses have warned him against having favorites, but Miguel can't help getting attached to the brave young boy who's fighting for his life. Besides, Zach's going to get well . . . isn't he?

Coming in April 2000!